VIKING ADVENTURES
HUGO CABRET CLASS 2021

Contents

Created   with   Vellum

Foreword

by Steve Higgs

I have read that there is no greater agony than trying to hold an untold story inside yourself. As a writer producing multiple novels a year, it is certainly something I can attest to, yet I find myself wondering how many of the people I pass in the street would also agree. Do they find themselves locked in a battle they would win if they only knew how?

There is something delicious about staring at the blank screen and knowing it is about to be filled with words. Capturing the essence of adventure or romance, sowing a seed on page four that will finally flourish as the sleuth sees the truth in the penultimate chapter. Describing lightning not by telling the reader that is what the character can see, but by filling their brain with a kaleidoscope of mesmerising light so blinding that they flinch - that is the opportunity that lies ahead for anyone who wishes to be a writer.

Through our words we can explore who we are. We can address our fears and overcome our weaknesses. Through words we can bring colour and joy, or evil and spiteful horror. Words have such power, and once they have been read by someone else, they are forever.

You are no doubt wondering who I am. The simple answer is that I am a person who makes their living by writing stories and whose eldest child just happens to attend St Mark's school.

My career as a writer started when the ten-year-old version of me won a writing competition. Were it not for that event, I might never have realised what could be. It was with that in mind that I approached the headmaster earlier this year.

With a view to inspiring the children in year six to also consider what might be possible, I showed them what I had done, and challenged them to unleash their imaginations.

I will admit that I had no idea what to expect but was pleasantly surprised by the depth and diversity they were able to display, and the colourful descriptive ability breathing life to many of their stories. Like alchemists, they turned one thing into another, but instead of lead into gold, they made the world in their head into words.

It is a beautiful thing to behold.

I am not suggesting that anyone should alter their life plans and instantly pursue a career as the next JK Rowling or James Patterson, however if a person enjoys writing stories, there are worse hobbies to have.

I committed to picking a winner and two runners up. Their stories are the first three you will come to. All others are entered alphabetically. I opted, right or wrong, to leave the children's work unedited. It is my belief that should they wish to look back many years from now, when their first novel wins the Booker Prize, they might enjoy seeing how far they have come.

Steve   Higgs

Echo's Adventure

by Lotanna Udolisa

In the corner of a gravel-pathed alleyway sat Echo – a young girl who'd just woken up to the mutterings of a peace treaty. "I heard that they're sending the Anglo-saxons a peace treaty!" said Mrs Carter the baker.

"Really?" asked Mr Carter, confused. "They're the ones who tried to burn down our houses the other week! Why do we have to send a peace treaty?"

Echo sat up straight as her ears perked up at the possibility of a peace treaty. After deftly buttoning up her shirt and searching through her hair for dirt, Echo promptly stood up and started walking towards the chief – her adoptive father.

Reaching the Viking longhouse, Echo knocked the door and stepped inside. The longhouse was littered with bones, animal skins and the remains of pheasant.

"Hello, Echo!" Shouted Vormamoo the Viking chief.

"Hello dad! Quick question… can I pretty, pretty, pretty please go on the voyage to send the peace treaty?" Echo asked with puppy eyes.

"No!" The chief's warm smile had now dropped and a frown crept up the sides of his face. "You're too young. You can look at the boat but not go on the journey!"

Just like that Echo was ushered out, but she had a plan she always had a plan.

Night rose from below the horizon and everyone was asleep, at least everyone except for Echo. Watching. her steps, Echo tip-toed down the lifeless streets of Viking town. She knew the peace treaty was heavily guarded. So she would have to send a friend to make a distraction, then she immediately stopped in her tracks. "I have no friends!" she thought, whilst realising her life was quite depressing. "I'll have to use one of their many weaknesses." She neared the longhouse where the treaty was kept and shouted "Free pheasant pie at the bakery!" A rampage of large, bulky and hairy Vikings stormed out as soon as Echo said that. Just to be sure, she checked inside before stepping in. It was a large room with no furniture except a glowing, misty box in the middle of the room. The box was large and had a leather flap over the top. Echo moved towards it warily, but seconds after she heard the stomps coming back to the room. She jumped in the dark interior of the glowing, ominous box and thought about how to get out of this predicament.

Hours passed and Echo's bottom felt a bit sore. She shuffled about until something rather large and abnormally heavy fell on her leg.

"Ow!" She screamed.

Suddenly, the leather flap was lifted offand she was met with two familiar faces.

"Kroggy and Frognuts!" Echo welcomed feebly.

Kroggy and Frognuts are brothers to Vormamoo and Echo's uncles. They were identical twins meaning that it's impossible to tell them apart if you don't know them. They had thick eyebrows and wore animal skins. They usually had swords with them –

the sign of great Viking warriors - but they didn't today.

"Echo! You should not be here! We're telling your father about this when we get back!" shouted Kroggy.

"When we get back? What do you mea-" She began to say, looking at her location.

She was no longer at Viking town, she was now on a bright-red boat heading towards Longship city – Viking town's sworn enemies the Anglo-saxons. Kroggy disconnected himself from the conversation focusing on the journey ahead.

"Wha-… how?" she managed to say. She started to stumble over her words and her feet too. She landed back on her bottom inside the metal box, hitting the object that injured her in her confinement earlier.

"Ow!" she cried again.

Echo checked the box and saw a stone hammer and the peace treaty. Influenced by her childish nature, Echo picked up the hammer and swung it around. "Why'd you have a hammer in here?" she asked.

"To defend ourselves in case of a battle, of course." Frognuts answered.

"Cool!" Echo stated.

"What? Nothing is cool! Nothing should be–" Kroggy interrupted, tuning back into the conversation.

But it was too late.

The hammer turned a flashing dark-blue as lightning escaped the metal container. Grey clouds swirled overhead. Words projected from the hammer into the sky reading: "You are the new Thor"

Soon after, the monarch of Longship city floated through the air, moving towards the boat at the speed of… lightning.

"He's flying!" Echo exclaimed.

"We know that!" Frognuts and Kroggy answered in unison. "Look, Echo that hammer belonged to Thor, God of Thunder, and you have been chosen to be the new Thor."

"You're joking right?" She chuckled nervously.

"We are Thor's angels. We have watched you from up to this point, protecting you as your dad's brothers. Now it is up to you and that stone hammer, Mjolnir, to go the rest of the way. Oh…heads up the Longship city chief, Lakun is trying to kill you. Bye!"

As soon as they revealed their angelic truth, Kroggy and frognuts started changing, shifting into golden dust making their ascent to Valhalla.

Echo needed time to digest what had just happened.

"Wha- I mean, come on!" She spluttered.

Seconds later, Lakun flew violently above the very boat Echo was standing in. With the lift of his arm the sea rose or descended. Lakun made shapes with his hands impossible to make by any human. The boat shuddered. Vibrations from the hull of the ship lifted to the small mast. Water crashed against the boat swaying it violently from side to side. That's when Echo saw it. Water was slowly surrounding the boat causing it to submerge with the sea.

Echo tried to escape the impending doom but it was fast and blocking any means of survival. Then in one fell swoop Echo and the boat descended through the dark-blue sea. She struggled and gasped for air but underwater it just caused more asphyxiation. "Oh Thor," she prayed "I've done nothing but been reckless. I was the one who wanted to come on this boat…Vormamoo warned me not to and I disobeyed his orders. I deserve this awful fate." And with that she closed her eyes. Then she felt a tug. A pull of upwards thrust was carrying her through layers of the deep sea. She looked up confused, then saw the greatest sight of her life.

"Mjolnir!" she tried to shout but instead swallowed a mouthful of seawater. Echo finally stopped at the surface of the sea and emptied her lungs of water. Suddenly, a projection flew up and out of the hammer. Sat in the middle was a man who had godly shoulders.

"Thor?" she asked.

"Yes, tis I. I have come to help you. Mjolnir isn't just a weapon it is your best friend. It is support where you need it and helps control your powers".

"Powers?" she asked.

"Yes powers," Thor answered.

"You are the god of thunder and with that, is powers and responsibility. As Thor can't take sides you can only ever even them".

"I've been meaning to ask you this…" Echo began.

"Since I'm adopted, Vormamoo isn't my real father. I'm the goddess of thunder and… you're the god of thunder. Meaning we have to be related somehow. Are you my…Ahem… Father?

…

7

"Thor?" Echo called.

…

"Hello earth to Thor?" she called.

…

"It doesn't matter anyway" she sulked.

"Yes, now go!" Thor demanded.

Thor's face spirited away with projection as it went back into the hammer.

Fuelled by the findings of her father, she swung Mjolnir round charging it and herself with immense amounts of power and shouted…

"I…am…Thor!".

She had finally become the hero she was meant to be.

Her eyes started glowing, flowing with electricity as her body was cocooned in luminescent lighting. She winced a little but then she eased into it as she saw it solidify. Thor's armour! She thought to herself. The 11-year-old had now turned into a warrior goddess covered in gold mythical armour. Echo looked for Lakun but he was nowhere to be seen until she turned around and saw Viking town. It was frozen in a box of ice. A frown slowly formed at the bottom of her face as Mjolnir lifted her up into the air. She flew. She didn't know how, but she did. She saw her cold environment and the blurs of seagulls, even the ripples she made on the surface of the water as she zoomed past. The small, icy squarc she saw from Longship Island had now turned into a gargantuan cube. She'd reached her destination.

"I take it you've seen the remnants of Viking town?". Said a gruff voice behind her.

Echo turned around and saw Chief Lakun but not the one she knew. His body was plagued with icy stalagmite, his complexion a sea-blue and his eyes were filled with ice and cold. Echo charged at Lakun, with Mjolnir in hand, but he merely side-stepped and Echo lost control, falling to the ground.

Red, saturated liquids flew out of her side, flowing through the gravel-pathed ground.

"Done already, I expected more from you!", Lakun teased.

She bounced back up grunting nonetheless, and threw Mjolnir with all her might at Lakun catching his cheek. That's when her attacks started to becoming more strategic". Every time Lakun side-stepped she attacked midway until… She flew up to the chief and something took over, a deep power grew from her stomach until it finally went to her chest, arms and then Mjolnir. Then her whole body starting glowing. A blast flew from Mjolnir striking Lakun and the ice that froze the town, but as soon as the blast fired off she realised Lakun had gone and so had his magic. So instead of hitting the hitting the ice the lightning-bolt hit a longhouse… one that looked quite familiar. She hit…chief Vormamoo. Echo's glow faded and she took off her gold armour. She sobbed and soon heard a voice that sounded godly.

"I'm sorry my child".

Then   the   two   Thors'   hugged.

Vic's Adventure

by Imogen Meredith

With sleep in his weary eyes, Vic was startled as his father awoke him. Vic's mind raced, chaos seemed to be erupting from outside. Screams filled his ears along with coughs and splutters from the chief's villagers. Smoke descended onto Vic and a charcoal smell filled his nostrils. From where Vic's father had stood him; he could feel a waft of heat and see villagers running past his door trying to find safety, while his father was frantically grabbing clothes and shoving them into a sheepskin bag. "What's going on?" asked Vic. "We need to escape now." replied his father. Hastily, his father picked Vic up and ran outside. Fire! It was everywhere. Another Viking tribe had arrived. "Everyone to the boats!" suddenly command the chief (as loud as possible). Vic was petrified. Even though, Vic was not the smartest boy, he knew it would be hard to carry on after this. What would they do?

Out of nowhere, the chief's wife screamed out, "Where's my daughter!" Tears ran down her cheeks in devastation. They had no time, Ordria (the girl) had vanished. Anxiously, her mum still ran on to the old, wooden boat. Soon everybody was there and the enemy had disappeared. Vic had a thought! "She was probably kidnapped," Vic announced, without thinking. "My sweet girl." cried the upset and worried mother. The chief pulled out a map (with no fuss) and started to find the other tribe's island. "There. Got it!" shouted out the chief. Everybody started hoisting anchors up knowing they were off to find Ordria. As Vic watched his home burn down, they set sail soon to arrive at another Viking home... Days were rough, storms kept occurring. Food nearly came to an end and Vic and his father were exhausted from helping on the ship every day. However, finally they could see their destination in view, ready to attack- stronger than ever.

With the plan all set out, they quietly lowered the anchors and stepped onto land for the first time in a week. "Yes," they all whispered. Silently, they walked on ready to find Ordria. Crunch, crunch, crunch! "Who was that?" murmured Vic... Out of nowhere, the other terrible tribe appeared out of the towering trees. "Found you!" laughed the Vikings like it was a game of hide and seek. "We want Ordria!" they commanded at once. Without a reply, the enemy set ablaze the dry ground with their large torches. Quite quickly the majestic trees turned ashen. Vic's mouth became dry. Heat spread everywhere it felt like it would never end! Vic whispered, "Use our drinking water and put it out." "Yes Vic!" murmured his father. Nature seemed to be on Vic's side as in that moment rain poured hard onto the expanding fire. His heart steadily, stopped pounding out of his chest. Every Viking cheered, nature had solved their problem. Now Ordria needed saving!

Fleeing from the havoc that had been caused, the undefeated people tip-toed on looking for the missing girl. When everything looked clear, the opposition mysteriously appeared. However, now they had brought weapons. "What now!" bellowed the chief. "Fight us," ordered the other vicious tribe. As quick as possible the young and old clutched the steel swords and axes ready for a brutal battle. "Attack!" yelled out the chief. Steel work hit metal in a matter of seconds. Vic went in to battle with an older-looking boy. He shouted a battle cry and started to fell butterflies growing inside his small stomach, while the other boy went on looking fearless. Without warning, the older boy lobbed Vic to the ground. The Vikings reformed ready to bring Ordria back to home. "AAhhh!" cried out the tired army. Feeling nervous, the opposition decided it was too risky so as fast as a flash they fled. Vic saw them running away, into their wooden, rickety boats. "Yes!" shouted the Viking group. Victory (and the girl) was theirs.

After a brief celebration, the Vikings carried on without fleeing uneasy about who else was on the island. "I know. Let's spilt up into three groups." started the chief. "We can find my daughter quicker that way." With a sparkle of hope in his eye, he split everybody up and mapped out where everybody was meant to go. "Yell as loud as possible, if you find her" expanded the chief. Vic and his father had been put in charge of the west group. Setting off from the others, their eyes scanned high and low like a security camera. Out of nowhere, a grizzly bear appeared. "WHAttt!" shouted Vic as a nervous shiver ran down his spine. "Help me!" cried out a worried voice. Vic questioned, "Ordria is that you?". Before the person could reply, the towering bear tried to scratch Vic. Suddenly, his father picked Vic up and out of the way. "It is Ordria," exclaimed his father before shouting as loud as possible to get the other groups attention. Before they knew it the others had arrived. "Mum, dad!" cried Ordria, a little bewildered. "Hi," called out her mother as tears of joy streamed down her face. "Only one problem," mumbled Vic's father, under his sigh. "What?" asked the confused chief. The bear hurled towards them. "AHHahhh!" yelled out everyone. "There is the problem," sighed Vic's father. "We have to scare it. Do anything you can!" explained Vic. "1,2,3 GO," he carried on. On 3 swords were drawn and others shouted or threw twigs. Terrified, the now scared grizzly bear turned and ran. They had done it again...

As the terrific tribe approached the girl, they discovered it was simple to get her out as it was just a dirt hole. "We could heave her out," suggested Vic, smiling from ear to ear; knowing he had come up with lots of ideas for them to achieve the journey at hand. His father assisted the chief and carefully hauled Ordria up, onto the grass once again. "I know we should be happy again b-b-but..." Vic stuttered. "But what Vic," replied his father. "Where is our new home?" asked Vic. Ordria moaned, "Yes we are village-less." Then an image flashed inside her father's head. "This is our new home." He remarked. Vic sighed with relief, "Yeah they fled from here." "How about we stay and migrate into their village," explained a Viking teenage girl. The chief exclaimed, "Yes, let's go find it!" As the group set off, they all thought of their new homes. How would they decorate their advanced village? In the trees, birds flew and the salty sea-water could be heard crashing into the jagged rocks. In the distance, the logs started to appear, then it revealed houses! Children ran towards their new chapter of life. Their new home was even better than their last.

Smiles were contagious around the people. Arms linked, loud and quiet songs were played. Vic felt heroic, nobody had given more thought on the entire journey. Himself and Ordria had become inseparable since she had been pulled from the dirt hole. One by one homes were chosen and plants were placed. Long-ships were positioned in the harbour standing on the water pride of place in their new location. After houses were renovated (to peoples tastes with bunting and more) homes had a family to look after. Everybody gathered in the middle of the vast village to celebrate and enjoy Ordria being back with them but also a wonderful island to live on. Trees had given shade over everyone, and parties carried on through the breeze of the midnight sky.

Scarlet's Adventure

by Seren Matthews

Jumping out of her uncomfortable, wooden bed, Scarlet ran to the door and opened it hastily. She heard the strong, ear-deafening bellow of the horn echo throughout the dull lifeless village. Scarlet stepped out of her house, wet air touched her pink cheeks. She smelled the smoke-filled air, it went up her nostrils and the cold breeze brushed against her brown, beach wavy hair. At this time, she was the only one outside. Scarlet sat on the leaf-filled wells edge and threw stones ferociously on the ground, she tapped her foot gently on the side in a beautiful beat. There wasn't any life here, no nature, just dull and dark. The small bridge is broken it has been for years now. Scarlet jumped off the edge of the well.

"Wake up lazy people!" Scarlet shouted to everyone in the village, 'Its 7am. Did you all not hear the horn?''.

Scarlet heard the distant, horrifying scream from her father's longhouse. Like a bullet, she ran into the wooden longhouse as sweat trickled down her forehead. She asked, ''What's wrong? And where is mum?''.

Her worried father said, ''She is g-gone. I think she has been kidnapped.''

Scarlet couldn't believe what was happening, she started to tremble and went pale. As she searched the house, she found an unusual note. It read 'Come find your mother she is on a mysterious island. In 5 days, she will be gone.' She couldn't believe what it read. Scarlet ran to her best friends (Veronica) house. After Scarlet informed her about what happened, they collected some bits to help them and got their dads and uncles, they climbed on a boat. Scarlet's father exclaimed, ''Go to the island that is in the shape of a Viking sword, go now!''.

Veronica's strong dad pushed the boat carefully away from the shore and they were off to the island!

Rumbling and cracking, thunder shook the boat and the waves were brutal. Scarlets determined father strived to keep the boat upright, his face was red and he was sweaty, he was holding on as tight as he could. Veronica and Scarlet were counting the seconds in-between each rumble, it was 20 seconds, then 15 and then it was 10! Out of nowhere, a strike of lightning illuminated the dark sky as rain drenched them. It smelled damp and smoky. Veronica shouted, ''Why did this have to happen? This is so petrifying!''.

Scarlet could barely hear what she said as the thunder overtook her words. The red and white sail had holes pierced through and was flapping in the howling wind. Scarlet's heart leapt out of her chest as her imagination ran wild. The rain drenched the group of 9.

After 20 minutes of constant horrible rain, it finally stopped. Scarlet looked around and stood up for the first time in a while. Her dad shrieked. Scarlet exclaimed, 'What's wrong d...''.

She saw it. In the foggy, far distance, there was a Viking longboat, a blue sail and a team of chanting

Vikings, cannons shot through the fog. The other troop started to get very close. Scarlets brave uncle (Uncle Mark) opened a crate and got: swords, shields and helmets out. They were ready for battle. Furiously, the other tribe ran onto Scarlet's dads boat and started to fight. Swords swung from side to side and they collided in the middle, growls were heard from all different directions from the longboat. Unable to do any damage, they ran back onto their own boat and fired cannons and sharp arrows. Then finally, they fled, after eventually they achieved some damage.

As the other troop finally went away, the team only just realised how much damage was actually done by the other Vikings. The rope that held the logs together were just falling apart, the red and white sail was ripped all over. Out of nowhere, the boat went under, it ripped in two. They all jumped off. Scarlet and Veronica were scared, their pulses raced as sweat dripped down their heads.

''How are we supposed to find her now?'' Scarlet screamed with water in her mouth.

Everyone didn't say a word.

"It's unfair, UGH.'' Scarlet had tears rolling down her cheeks like Olympic runners racing.

No one could see Scarlet as darkness enveloped their eyes. Suddenly, Veronica was crying but no one heard her. The birds stopped squawking, the waves were calm. Scarlet's father shouted, ''Swim! There's an island we can go to shore.''.

Leaving their boats wreckage behind, they all paddled to the shore of the unknown island. They all went to sleep on the sand that night.

As the sun woke, the group was rubbing their water eyes as they sat up and yawned away. Scarlet exclaimed, ''Right. I guess we need to somehow make a new boat to get to the island''.

Scarlets dad mumbled, '' No,'' everyone looked at him, ''We are here! This is the island.''

Veronica was shocked. Scarlet shouted, ''What are we doing just stand here, let's go!''.

After hours of nonstop looking, they found a cave. Without saying a word, Scarlets father barged in. He picked up a ring from the ground with a ruby embodied in it. Scarlet recognised it, she thought for a moment, it was her mothers. Her mum's scream was trapped inside of the eerie cave. As they walked further in, Scarlet was looking at the walls of the cave they had markings carved in them. They saw her. She was trapped in a steel cage. Scarlets dad opened the door with his sword. She was out. Scarlet hugged her mum, then the troop ran as quick as they could back to their spot they slept the night before.

After a while, the group finally got to the spot they slept the night before. Scarlet felt so heroic as she led the team to a fantastic victory (finding her mum). Scarlet's dad exclaimed, "Joanne we are really happy to have you back.'' Everyone nodded in agreement, "but we don't have a boat!''. Vic (scarlets dad) looked around and everyone was awkwardly smiling. They got to work, Scarlet was swinging axes, tying logs and making a sail. It was done, after 2 hours of hard work. Then they set sail, the sea was much calmer this time. Scarlet steered the boat around the jagged rocks. Finally, they got home. There was a feast waiting for them. Scarlet was thrown up in the air with Veronica. Suddenly, the chief bellowed, ''Can I have your attention. Can we please clap for veronica and scarlet as they saved Joanne, Also, they get their golden helmets!'' Scarlet had a powerful smile on her face and she stood with her shoulders back. She was also given a sword and Veronica was given a massive axe.

They were now proper Vikings.

Hiccup's Adventure

by Cody Attubato

It was a lovely day and Hiccup and Stoak prepared a feast for the village. When they were eating all of a sudden a lightning bolt hit Stoaks' wife, Valcaree. Whilst Hiccup was watching Astrid (his crush) the lightning disturbed his thoughts and created a fire causing a Viking to throw their rum on it.

Hiccup and his dad hurried to speak to the oldest and wisest person in the village. Once they got to the hut, the old lady gasped "What happened to her? I haven't seen anything like this and trust me I have experienced lots before. How did this happen? "Stoak replied "A lightning bolt hit her" trying to hold back his tears. You must go to the mountain before the ice freezes over, hurry you need to speak to the gods to turn her back to normal.

So Hiccup and his father rushed up there only taking a lantern and Valcaree (Hiccups mum). It was a long journey all the way to the top it, was tiring and draining but they eventually got there. Stoak shouted "Help me turn my wife back to normal from this electricity ball!".

Zeus exclaimed "Bring me your finest sheep and I'll do just that". With a click of his fingers they looked around and were back in their village.

Then Stoak quickly remembered that all the sheep had been stolen 1 week ago, so they set sail to go to a market on another island. They rowed and rowed and they eventually got there after a whole night of rowing. They rushed to the farmer and said "We would like to buy your finest sheep". He went to the back of the barn and showed them the sheep. Stoak told him that that will do the job, so Stoak brought a single sheep.

As Stoak was bringing the sheep to the dock, he noticed his ship was sinking and it had ginormous holes in the side, he rushed to the ship seller to buy a new ship but he said "Sorry, I just sold my last one".

Then out of nowhere Hadies appeared in front of Stoak and told them "I have been watching you for weeks now and it looks like you need help getting back to your island, hold on to me". They teleported to the top of the mountain and Hadies called to Zeus, "They're here and they have brought a sheep." Zeus zapped Valcaree and she turned back into a woman again.

They decided to have another feast but this time Stoak said "This time we should have it inside".

Oscar's Adventure

by Elijah Anscomb

Tired and scared, Oscar woke up hearing a strange unknown screeching sound that pierced his ears. Hastily, he jumped out of bed as goose bumps assembled on his arms and finally the sound had stopped. He walked through the crooked hallway as dead silence surrounded the village. A cold breeze tingled on his hairs whilst he ran to the muddy squelchy, pathway. Oscar saw a dark cloaked figure walk up the pathway heading straight for the abandoned, isolated cliffs. Mist enveloped him blocking his vision. Where did the dark ghost go? He thought trembling in fear. "Who are you?" echoed Oscar as he was worried and confused. Quickly, he ran up the chalky cliffs wondering if it was a new sign of life. Then he came face to face with a gloomy, pitch-black cave shaped like a mouth. Without hesitation, he bolted in making himself a less easy target. But there was no ghost just a big titanium hammer with rune markings across its wooden engraved handle. Oscar clutched onto the hammer with all his might and tried to pick it up, it was easy. Blue shimmering lights formed around him. "You are Thor's descendant," bellowed a loud voice.

Suddenly, a large boom shook the village, as Oscar could hear screams of terror that travelled on for miles. Looking back, he pointed the hammer at the burning houses as he had heard stories of Thor's hammer using water. Nothing happened. Then at once a large rain cloud floated above them sending powerful rain down on to the houses which were burning undefeatably. Oscar ran to the village shouting for his dad. "Oscar we have got to go," shouted his father. "Why? I like home." Then his dad explained about an evil rival named Ivan Fireball who had a magic arm, which could only be stopped by someone worthy of Thor's hammer, "Dad I think that is me," confessed Oscar "Then we shall set sail immediately." Oscar climbed up onto the boat and rose the sails as his dad shouted "Helheim here we come." They had been sailing for about an hour when they heard a strange, mystical roar...

Recognising the creatures roar, Oscars dad knew it wasn't a Punbeetle or a Jangbee but the strongest creature of all, an Alpha Romeo. Sharp, red and jagged spikes cut the water as the monster charged for the weak boat. Oscar's heart thumped rapidly whilst his emotions switched dramatically. The monster swung its tail at the boat making a long wide cut and knocking the boat aside. Amazingly, the creature had a scaly exo-skeleton, katana sharp teeth, large flaming nostrils and two highly developed green beady eyes. Its tail was one deadly spike that could pierce healthy bones and adapted muscles. Oscar was frozen. He was powerless against this humongous beast. Until he realised the beast had no heart, as it wasn't producing blood from its cuts. "Dad crash into its chest," screamed Oscar. His dad skidded the boat around trying to make the time right. Oscar shot the lightning bolt down as his dad crashed into its outer exo-skeleton, destroying the monsters' protection. The monsters gaping mouth roared once more and dived into the oceans deep-blue depths.

Oscar and his father sailed on through the thunderous weather and burning lightning with a hole emerging in their ship. Luckily, Oscars dad was a professional blacksmith so he repaired it with ease. Waves grew up like people, as the water splashed onto the ragged deck. Without warning, a skyscraper wave towered over them dropping at ferocious speed. This wave was confident and bold using all its might. Then, it hit the ship dragging it down and down and down into a dark frightening abyss, like an anchor. A secret tunnel thought Oscar? A long narrow stream leading to a fiery castle, that hung amongst everything. But as soon as they figured where they were, enemy ships surrounded them. Oscar and his dad knew the ships were for one thing and one thing only, to kill outsiders. In a flash, a firebomb came raging at them dealing a fatal blow to the ship. "Quickly, jump onto the enemy boat," screamed Oscars dad in pain from the stinging burn marks. Oscar was trained. He could beat them. Swords came crashing down as Oscar clutched the hammer and pounded the deck, splitting the adapted boat in halve. Enemies fell into the hot, scorching river whilst Oscar jumped onto the magma stairs. Oscar walked up the sun-coloured steps as his dad limped behind him. Fierce, angry fighters blocked the doorway but were no match for Thor's hammer which crushed their bones and ripped their muscles, "Nice to see you again," cackled Ivan "Are you going to fight me or not?" His majestic hand shone bright, revealing its power, shooting fire shards at the trembling duo.

Oscar pushed his dad aside and dived with him, but Ivan picked them up and threw them against the wall. "Your no match for my greatness," murmured Ivan. Oscar knew he was big-headed and thought only the best of himself, so he tried to distract him away from his dad. Oscar shot a lightning bolt down, as Ivan barely dodged it but still jumped back up! The hammer floated out of Oscars hand and threw itself at the arm. "No don't leave," bellowed Oscar. Crash! Walls started to collapse and the floor began to give way. The arm held the power of Helheim. Ivan fell to his knees as Oscars dad grabbed his trustworthy sword and plunged it deep into Ivan's heart. Broad shoulders, glistening eyes and a joyful smile rose heroically as lightning struck them; sending the two excited men back to their loved village.

They had finally returned home. Surprisingly, villagers knew what happened and praised Oscar. "Welcome home, your just in time for a scrumptious feast," explained Bogtrotter, the village cook. "Lets' eat," exclaimed Oscar. The variety was huge as Oscar licked his lips waiting in anticipation for the delicious juicy meat to be served. "This gathering is for Oscar and his skilled dad," shouted Pete. Oscar blushed and a glamorous smile spread across his face knowing he saved multiple villages. Now there was no Ivan so people could live freely and safely and spend time with their friends and family. Oscar missed the hammer but at that moment it appeared in his hands making him feel like it will always be by his side. Oscar proudly boomed, "To the downfall of Helheim,"; or will it come back?

Lis's Adventure

by Eliza Scadeng

One morning something very terrible happened, the king's daughter went missing. Normally Lis, the kings' daughter, is the first one up! Vikings awoke and no one has seen Lis yet? The king asked his son to go see if she was still asleep, but she had disappeared.

"The kings' daughter is missing", shouted the kings' son.

The king ordered a search party immediately.

Suddenly King Vick heard a scream of terror.

"Where is my daughter", shouted King Vick.

The Vikings shouted from the top of their voices in panic.

"Our enemies, they have got her because of her special powers".

Everything Lis touches turns into gold. King Vick spotted something.

"What's that George?" said the king.

"It's a letter" replied George.

"What does it say?" shouted king Vic.

"It's from King Fesle" said George.

George said, "We have got a mission to go on, but we must go now, we have only got twenty-four hours to get Princess Lis back".

So off they went on their mission.

"Forty villagers on each boat" shouted king Vick.

As the sixty boats left shore, George whispered to the king "Don't worry, we will get Lis back."

With a sound the Vikings had never heard before, coming from beneath them, in the depths of the sea, out from the smooth surface of the sea, all of a sudden a massive green slimy octopus like creature took chunks off of their boat as it wrapped its tentacles around the sinking boat. The villagers began to cut off its tentacles with their shining swords, while flying cannons tore its flesh, it began to slowly sink down into the red blood sea.

Sea crashing against the rocks, wind whistling the boats rocked side to side. The king screamed "I can see enemy island in the distance, Oh No a tornado ahead!".

Into the tornado they went, it gobbled them up like we gobble our favourite food. Round and round they went like a roller-coaster no way to get out, nowhere to go. Holding on for their lives after an hour or more, the tornado stopped, their boat had sunk and they only had logs left, two or six Vikings holding on each.

"We will not give up" said the king.

So they didn't give up, they found some of their weapons floating whilst getting closer to the enemy island.

Arriving at the enemy island, battle started, swords being waved about, cannons flying. It was not safe for the kids so they sent them off with the best girl Viking, Charle, to look after the them. After a while they found princess Lis, she was locked in a cage, with a small Viking, sleeping by door. They saw the key on the Vikings belt, they crept up and stole it. But around the corner three fat Vikings were charging at them. Charle saw them and shouted "Run, meet me back at the logs".

So they run as fast as they could, their little hearts pounding like a drum, they got to the logs and started to paddle. Charle screamed "Wait", as she jumped as far as she could on to one of the logs.

Princess Lis said "What about my dad?".

"He will be ok," Charle replied, as she stroked her head to comfort her.

With a couple of hours gone, the Viking's arrived at their island, injured.

After several hours, the whole village celebrated with food, music and dancing. Celebrating getting Lis back and defeating king Fesel and his Vikings. The sound of children playing and them running around, the smell of all of that food cooking, music blearing in their ears, the Vikings partied all night and slept all day.

Everything went back to normal, Lis was still the first one up and Green Field island lived happily ever after… for a couple of months that is, until the enemy island started to steal all of their food!

Odinia and Marcus' Adventure

by Emelia Harrup

Odinia slowly opened her eyes to the sound of her father's voice and then awoke with a start. When she walked outside silence filled the air and the only person there was her father who had now become quiet. Arrows stuck out of village houses and smoulder filled the air. Looking through the smoulder Odinia immediately sensed there had been a raid.

"Dad what has happened?" questioned Odinia. Her father looked down with disappointment and didn't say a word. His face had shown it all. Odinia wanted desperately to find her friend Marcus, but knew he would still be in a deep sleep. She walked outside alone in the eerie village. Flames danced in torches and the village felt abandoned, with nobody inside.

Suddenly, a yell could be heard and Odinia jumped, thinking there was an attack, just to see an old Viking warrior shouting, "The jewel, the jewel, its missing, everybody, wake up now!" Marcus appeared slowly out of his longhouse with messy hair and sleepy eyes. Odinia sprinted over and whispered to him that the historic jewel was missing. He gasped and pointed to a huge longboat in the distance, fading away into the misty air. She knew that Marcus was thinking the same as her when a horn blew and a fire ball headed straight for them. Loud ear piercing screams filled their ears and then a huge crash!

Feeling a hard shove, Odinia tumbled to the ground next to Marcus. Her father (the chief) had pushed her out the way of the fire ball. Odinia quickly thanked him just before the raid started again. Silently, Odinia pulled Marcus onto a wooden longboat, covering his face before he screamed. As fast as possible, Odinia explained "I had to sneak out otherwise the jewel would be lost forever!". Marcus nodded and while they attempted to figure out a plan a huge longboat came closer and closer. Before they could even blink, armed enemy Vikings surrounded them with swords, shields and axes. Odinia and Marcus froze, as though their feet were stuck with glue, to the wood. They had no idea what to do…

Bravely, Odinia used her sword and fought the enemies away and she sailed the longboat forward using a dusty map lying on the boat. The sky turned a gloomy grey and dark black clouds floated up high. A little droplet of rain landed on the boat and Marcus looked at her, Odinia shrugged and turned the sail left. All of a sudden, rain poured out the sky drenching the children in dirty rain water. Thinking it couldn't get any worse the children put their hands over their heads and ducked down. In the sky, thunder cracked, then the boat shook aggressively rocking the children back and forth, then a strike of lightning hit the sail and the children screamed into the gloomy night.

Eventually the thunder settled, the two children were so relieved that the awful weather had gone but they hadn't noticed the water rising in the boat. While

Odinia was hugging Marcus she looked down and saw the turquoise water rising. Odinia exclaimed "Marcus look, the boat is sinking, quick help me!" Suddenly, the boat had sunk to the very bottom of the sea and all that was left was broken pieces of wood floating on top of the water. Leaving the children stuck at sea, the boat had now disappeared from sight. Now stranded, Odinia and Marcus swam to a nearby island not knowing what to do, they stepped onto the hot sand.

While the terrified children were on the island they saw a mysterious bump in the sand. After Odinia and Marcus helped each other dig it up, the most incredible jewel, that was missing, appeared! Footsteps could be heard so they both hid behind a towering palm tree and then the enemy Vikings walked by. They both gasped amazed as the enemies noticed the jewel was gone and growled angrily and went back to their caves. Odinia then thought of an idea to get back home. She used logs, twigs and crunchy leaves to make a small raft for them to travel home in. With a spring in their step they hopped onto the raft joyfully. While the sea crashed, Odinia gripped onto the jewel tightly, not risking for it to be lost again. "Marcus can you please control the boat I have been doing it for ages!" exclaimed Odinia. Before they even knew it the two children were fast asleep on the raft traveling onwards south.

Finally, the children saw the village and all the sadness drained from their faces as happiness filled their eyes. Standing taller, Odinia helped Marcus off the boat and cheers filled their ears. The chief ran through the crowd and pulled Odinia into a massive bear hug. "I can't believe you did it Odinia you are a true hero!" shouted her father. Marcus hugged his parents as they congratulated him excitedly. Smiles and hugs filled the village with endless joy. A long wooden table was between the crowd with so much celebration food on top. Overwhelmed, the children sat together at the table tucking into the food, starved from all the work they had done. Ten minutes later, all the food had gone and the entire village was full. The chief then bellowed "Everybody to celebrate Odinia and Marcus' return, we will have a dance party!" After all the dancing and laughter ended the Viking children said goodnight and fell into a deep deep   sleep...

Vickie's Adventure

by Emelia Allen

With a blurry vision in her eyes, Vickie woke up to hear the sound of loud men shouting as they prepared to have a battle. Without hesitation, Vickie jumped out of bed faster than lightning, with her legs wobbling and goose bumps climbing up her arms.

"Ugh what's going on out there?" Vickie groaned to herself as she heard her dad blowing the horn, making the ground rumble.

Vickie ran up to her bedroom window to see her dad (the Viking leader) lining up the men like soldiers standing to attention.

Suddenly, Vickie heard a big booming voice coming from outside of her house. She raced downstairs to see her parents and ten other Viking men standing in one big line. With confusion in her eyes, Vickie asked her parents, "Where are you going?"

"We are going to a Viking battle," Vickie's mum answered.

Vickie ran up to her parents, gave them a big hug and whispered to them good luck! Her parents and the other Vikings hopped into the boat and slowly drifted away. As her parents were sailing across the sea, an arrow hit them, the boat was damaged from flying fireballs, they disappeared under the water. Not long after, Vickie's parents found themselves on the land again. All the other men were still sleeping so the pair decided to wait for them to wake up. It had been hours now since Vickie's parents had left and she was getting worried. She thought to herself for a while and decided that she should wait a little bit longer, as she needed to think of a plan.

As the sun peeked through Vickie's bedroom window, she finally decided to go help her parents as she could sense trouble. She asked her friend Bailey to come and she said yes, she also got Baileys' dad to come too. They got into Baileys dads boat and sailed away into the direction of the way her parents went in. Luckily Vickie knew where the battlefield was and she led the way. As they were sailing Vickie spotted a miniature figure in the distance. Heading closer, she could see hundreds of different sea creatures blocking their way. In the blink of an eye, she told Bailey what she could see in front of her and Bailey told her dad, Ben. Ben quickly stopped the boat. Luckily on the boat were dead fish that Bailey thought that they could use as feed. Dark getting closer, Vickie threw the fish into the water hoping Baileys plan would work. It worked. The creatures scattered off into the distance. Suddenly, huge strikes of lightning burst into the air like fireworks exploding and the boat started to shake side to side. As it grew louder and louder, the girls became worried, Ben immediately stopped the boat and started shaking too. The storm continued to grow…

As the storm carried on, black smoke smothered the sky like a dull grey blanket. Out of nowhere, a huge whirling tornado whizzed around and around, crashing them into jagged boulders and abandoned wooden Viking boats all around them. Stranded in the middle of the ocean, with a damaged boat, but not letting water in! Vickie's heart beat leapt out of her chest and her arms shook dramatically.

Later, Ben, Bailey and Vickie awoke to see the sun shining again and the dark clouds no longer there.

Furiously, the vicious waves crashed over the boat and caused the sail to detach and fall into the depths of the ocean. SPLASH! They were gone. Vickie's heart dropped. There was no sail to guide the boat. All of a sudden Vickie, Bailey and Ben felt the boat going down, down, down. They were now each standing on the edge of the boat like they were hanging on the edge of a cliff. Suddenly, they heard a loud ear-piercing noise. A broken tree. Vickie constructed a plan. She quickly told Bailey and Ben. Soon, they tried to grab the gnarled old tree but the two girls were not strong enough. Ben achieved it on his own. Sweat dripping down his face, he pushed and pulled the long tree so they could all climb on. Ben had to take off his warm fluffy coat and use it for the sail of the new boat. Using the ores of the last boat they sailed away, hoping for no more problems.

As they were paddling, Bailey spotted an island with figures of people sitting on it. They sailed towards it. The Sun was setting and the night was getting close again. When they arrived on the island Vickie ran towards a person who strangely looked like her mum. Out of nowhere she saw her dad and the Viking crew standing in front of her. She couldn't believe it.

"I've missed you guys." Vickie said.

"We have missed you too." Vickie's dad said back.

They soon came to an agreement to stay until tomorrow before they go back home.

The next day, they woke up with huge grins on their faces ready to go back home. Soon, the crew set off on the tree and sailed back home.

Sun still shining, they arrived home. To their surprise, confetti exploded into the air like a bomb and food was scattered all over the table. Drums were being played and little kids were laughing and dancing to the music. Everyone was happy, even the wise old man who never smiles. Vickie felt proud and humble. People cheering her name. Not long after everybody was hungry, so they all went to the table which was full of fish, chicken and drinks.

Later that day, the party was still going and Vickie was thinking how she couldn't have saved her parents without Bailey and Ben.

Vickie was a real Viking hero!

Scarface's Adventure!

by Faye Millar

Barely able to open his eyes, Scarface heard deafening screams and screeches in the depths of the village. Quick as he could, he darted outside to see what the commotion was all about, then suddenly realized his father (The Viking leader Odin) was missing. Everyone was speechless as they froze with fear looking to see if he was in sight. Everyone's mouth gapped open, even Scarface and his mother. Rapidly, everybody searched all the crevices and cracks but still no sight of him. Scarface sighed. He was so confused; When and why did this happened? He wanted to get his father back but didn't know how!

Suddenly in the fog covered sky, Scarface saw a miniature figure drifting away. Disappearing slowly, he had a thought, imagine if it was his dad. At that moment, he realized it was his dad after what felt like an hour or so. Scarface immediately drew attention to the whole village and the tribe, so they set sail into the dark emerald ocean! After 5-10 minutes passed, they heard songs and weapons clashing. They were confused! Out of nowhere, they realized it was another Viking army and slowly something emerged from the thick fog!

"Prepare for war men," Scarface bellowed

With his heart pounding out of his chest, Scarface had no idea of what to do in the Viking longboat battle. Without warning, he was struck across the boat, he was badly injured!

"I need back up, help, help," Scarface wailed in pain.

Instantly, the backup came, they thunderously jumped onto the boat as it rocked side to side. Cautiously, the tribe searched the perimeter of the ship to see if they were endangered. All of the tribe thought it was safe but suddenly they heard a flurry of crashes and thuds and at that moment they knew they were in trouble, they needed an idea. A few minutes Later, they had thought of an attack, they patiently and slowly crept up behind the enemies...BANG, they were knocked out instantly.

"Is my dad there please, tell me he is?" Scarface exclaimed.

"He isn't, they must have hidden him at their base," A member of the tribe replied.

Later on, the tribe fixed Scarface's injury and for that reason they set sail into the depths of the ocean ready for anything that stood in their way!

Questioning himself, Scarface wondered how he was alive; he nearly broke his leg! Barely awake and having no idea where he was or where to go. Gradually, the tribe member controlling the boat was falling asleep, but Scarface, as confused as he was, had an eye on him.

"Wake up you lazy thing," Yelled Scarface.

"No, no, no I'm awake I think," replied the tribe member.

After the man awoke, they carried on going forward with their journey every dusk and dawn. Until one day, it was the middle of the night everyone was sound asleep, even Scarface, and out of nowhere…CRASH! The boat was hit by jagged rocks as they were perched on their thrones.

"What's going on men I'm getting damp," exclaimed Scarface.

"We are not doing that, who do you think we are," explained a tribe member.

Quick as a lightning bolt, Scarface noticed their long boat was sinking, the whole tribe, Scarface and his mum had to think of something quick! Without warning, people started to fall in seas and not many could swim!

"Grab an object and float in the ocean and if there is not enough share!" Scarface screamed. Stranded at sea, the tribe was starving and everyone was exhausted, they tried to get back to shore but the current was so strong they were useless against it. It would probably take a few days to get back to dry land. Every day that went by, they would move a metre but not all were lucky. Finally, they only needed one more good wave but that would still be hard to get in a current like this!

Will we ever get back to shore or even live through this?" Scarface Muttered

With a huge sigh of relief, some of the tribe, Scarface and his mum made it to dry land. They were still gutted they had not found Odin (Viking Leader) and due to that Scarface let the tribe rest and eat while he went on the hunt for his father. Around 15-20 minutes later, Scarface almost gave up but he kept striding forward to find his father. During his search, Scarface found a shovel in the middle of nowhere, so he decided to dig up the area to see what was there!

Slowly but surely, Scarface had shovelled up the area and without knowing a rock solid object was in the way. Cautiously, Scarface brushed the top of it and realized it was a human- sized container of some sort.

"Why is this so difficult to lift the lid?" whispered Scarface.

After a long period of time, Scarface managed to elevate the lid and suddenly realized it was his dad (The Viking Leader Odin).

"Dad it's you, but I must say your beard is fluffy," exclaimed Scarface.

"I knew you would find me," replied Odin.

Going further on with his journey, Scarface and his dad met back up with the tribe but they still needed a way back home.

"Calm down everyone you have been tricked because behind this massive hill is the village," shouted Odin.

Annoyed that they got tricked they still travelled back to the village. On their journey back they walked beside the gushing waves as they attacked the shore. Surprisingly, creatures from the depths of the blue ocean jumped with joy as they insisted for a ride and so they did. Gradually the tribe, Scarface and his mum had a joyful ride back home, enjoying the view of the village as the sun set slowly. After what felt like would never end, Scarface and the people from the rest of the village were a tiny bit frustrated that they had to jump off. Before midnight they made it back home,

"I'm dying out here, I'm starving please give me food," explained all of the tribe.

"Alright calm down you pigs, we will have a feast only because of Scarface saving me," replied Odin.

They celebrated with an enormous feast and everyone cheered. Scarface eyes glistened in the night as he sat up with his shoulders broad.

"Cheers to Scarface," bellowed Odin, as the whole tribe gave a toast to the mighty Scarface. Without awareness Scarface was added to the wall of leaders and was knighted as a god for what he achieved. That evening he strolled the shoreline alone, as he gazed into the starry night he stood tall and was filled with pride.

Harry's Adventure

by Harry Hedge

Hastily, Harry awoke to the sound of metal clattering, wood hitting and screams of pain. A battle had been going on. He grabbed his axe and shield and ran out just to have realised the disadvantage they had. The enemies had twice as many men out on their long ship. "Harry, oi Harry stay by the wheel in case of any sudden need of escape!" bellowed dad. "I'm on it!" Harry calmly exclaimed. He watched as their army went down and down in men until there was nobody left. Harry had to take out an enemy man and fled home, alone with nothing left except from blood and dead bodies for a crew.

After a few hours of nonstop fear running through his heart, Harry made it to the shore and all his fear vanished like a magician and a rabbit. Not surprisingly, the village was dead silent, giving it an abandoned feel to it. Harry found his house, sat down and went to bed, not willing to relive anything that happened that day. He woke up to the sound of others muttering. Harry wasn't alone. He yanked his axe, with no time for a shield, and went outside just to spot a boat leaving with all the good loot ever needed. After a few seconds Harry realised what had happened, he had been raided. He checked a few houses and almost everything had been robbed. Just seconds before they left, Harry grabbed a spyglass from his pocket and saw something utter terrible!

They had taken Odin's magical sword. Harry knew what he had to do. Get it back or die trying.

He stared at the boat for a minute, studying the appearance of it for when he finds their village. Without hesitation, Harry jumped onto the boat and hoisted the sails up. "I can't do this alone, I'll need some help," he whispered to himself. After a while, strong, black depths surrounded him and the boat. Long, navy tentacles arose through the deep, dark water. Quickly, Harry clutched onto his axe whilst his hearty raced rapidly. The kraken was here! It threw its tentacles onto the boat and held on tightly. In the blink of an eye, Harry gripped onto his axe and cut the tentacles into pieces. With one last high-pitched screech it fell into the abyss of the sea. Harry was safe but it won't be long before he isn't.

"Haha, unlucky kraken," Harry exclaimed to himself proudly. Harry looked up and realised this trip was going to be 10 times harder. The kraken had ripped off the sail and taken it down with him. Now Harry had to think hard, does he go back, go and find the enemy village, or go to the nearest island in hope for some human help. After some thinking the 3rd option sounded like the best option for him. Just minutes later an island had been located and he made his way. But obviously because of what happened to the sail this was not easy. The boat would barely do what you wanted from it and it was hard to control, but he still made it. Now all Harry needed to do was explore. Then he noticed what he never wanted to notice after a few minutes of walking. It was the boat he saw robbing him and Odin's magical sword. How could he get his sword back alone?

You wouldn't need to know because there were 2 other men from the enemy side who had just been kicked out, their faces bright red with rage wanting revenge." Hel-hel, hey cou- could you h-help me g-get my mag-magic sw-sword, Odin's sword," Harry stammered. "Of course young boy, I'd do anything to get vengeance on that horrible bunch of men," the first exclaimed. "I knew karma would come to bite them," the other added. "Just don't be too loud whilst trying to get it back, I know where they dug it," the first said, already on the go. As quiet as a mouse, they crept up slowly to the village, axes in hand. A lucky thing was that nobody had watched them walk out otherwise the plan would already be over. "They buried it behind the chief's house, won't be easy to get to, there are 2 guards protecting the front of it". "Luckily there's none at the back," the first chuckled. After a few minutes of sneaking they arrived around the back of the chief's house. "Now all we need is a shovel, you got one boy?" The second questioned. Oh god! Harry thought to himself. "I left it back on the boat," he quickly replied. "I'll get it, what direction is it in," the first decided." That way," Harry replied pointing in the direction of the boat. After around 7 minutes he came back and they began digging. It wasn't long before Harry hit something hard and saw the black and gold colours of the sword. He gave the men the shovel and held it majestically, feeling like he was a Viking god. "Should we get out of here, I can take you to my village," Harry asked. "Sure, why not," they both responded at the same time, "remember to be quiet."

Clack! Clack! Clack! It was the chief! "I thought I told you both to leave and die in Helheim, who's this and, wait, give that sword back!" the chief bellowed. Oh no we were in trouble.

Harry tried to run but knew it wouldn't work. He didn't want to do it but it was a matter of life and death. He slashed the chief down but it didn't kill him. It only froze him. Harry felt better knowing he didn't have to kill anyone. "Uuuhh, I think we should go," the first man whispered. They all ran back to the boat. Harry breathed heavily. "We might need a sail," Harry laughed. He remembered the spare sail and asked the second man to attach it, which he did perfectly and they all rode home.

Dear Diary, August 24th 1042

I'm 20 now and haven't used this thing since I was 6. It's been 10 years since my dad died and I'll never forget the moment, it's stuck in the back of my brain. If there is any way he can read this, I want to tell him. Hello dad, if you can read this, I lived on your legacy. I'm the leader even though I'm the youngest in my clan. I have won many battles just like you, your still my biggest inspiration. I found the warrior in me just how you wanted me too. I am one of the most feared leaders in Scandinavia. I did it dad. I'm just like you.

This was the last memory of Harry. He was never found again after the battle of Hastings.

Ullr's Great Battle

by Jake Wilkes

With a blurred vision and a sprinkle of nerve, Ullr
awoke huddled away like a baby to the stern, mighty
voice of the shanty singer singing "Norway, frost and
ice. Cold winds blowing. Land of Vikings Norway."
As he stood he saw his destination. England. Ullr
straightened himself to his feet with a sword in one
hand and a shield in the other. Helmet on. Chain
armour equipped. And a lantern on his belt for the
inky black night of Hastings.

As they tread on the sandy shore watching the
Anglo-Saxons charging towards them. "Get ready!"
Bellowed Ullr whilst he braced with his shield and
axe, sharpened teeth and forty more long-ships full of
warriors behind him…As the enemies approached
closer and closer, Ullr's father ran in front of him
barking like a stray dog spotting bread on the floor.
The Saxons ignored him barging the father away like
a tennis racket hitting a ball. "My chief! Your father.
He has been swarmed and swallowed like Tyr's arm
between Fenrir's gaping jaws!" worried one of the
warriors. "Come on and move men!" ordered Ullr.
The berserkers marched to the top of the hill colliding
with the other side… But Ullr's father was not in
sight. He had vanished into thin air.

With a father missing, Ullr tried to think of a
solution to dart out of the battle without his deceivers
noticing. He had a brainstorm to sprint to the nearest

cave system. They gradually move to the sullen cave and stay the night. The next morning a colossal explosion so deafening makes its appearance that they all jump up, some warriors injured from hits. Rocks piled, creating a barrier over the entrance, Ullr questioned to himself, when and how did this happen? "Good morning my friends." giggled Loki the Joker. "Loki, by Odin's thunder. Is that you?". Ullr stumbled before him tripping on an imposters rock. "That's my name." Charmed Loki sweetly. "By the way I know your father and where he is… Right now he is being tortured by my wonderful illusions" he added. "Tell me now!" Yelled Ullr. "Only if you fight me and my son", "You have a son!?" Muttered Ullr. "Fenrir a great beast. As a pup only five meters tall!" Loki crazily cackled. "I'm… well we are up for this quest" Ullr agreed. "Good, good" Loki crowed. And finally the fight began!

Loki whistled a high pitch frequency to summon Fenrir above all clouds. "My son, please would you accept this fight between you the great beast and them the weak and feeble crew to win their chained leader back?". "Of course master as long as they can defeat me to the death." bragged the beast. Fenrir did a warning howl to let the crew know it has begun. Ullr scattered around the cave's walls like a spider dodging a magazine as the crew took and gave immense hits to Fenrir. "Agh" yelped Loki and the wolf because they had a physical bond. Ullr grabbed his axe that was smothered in poison and took a blow to the head of the giant creature…

Shooting from the ground, a fiery tornado whipped all of Ullr's crew and he watched their souls leaving their poor bodies. The tornado shrivelled away like a tortoise cowering into its shell. As Fenrir rolls over with his father Loki, Ullr straightened his eyes to his father who was locked away like a memory box hidden away in the corner of the loft. "To Hell with you." Ullr quietly gasped from bites from the fiend as a gate of fire opened and sucked Loki and his son into the great beyond. A key was spat from Fenrir's parting jaws and landed in Ullr's withered hands shining like a beacon across the ocean.

"You've saved me!" Ullr's father shrieked in joy. Ullr inserted the key into the lock causing chains to flood out like tickets from an arcade machine. The father leaped out painfully from being cramped in one position. "We need to find a way out of here now! And never run off like that!" Ordered Ullr. They both pounded their axes at the rocks which were another hoax from Loki. "Oh that idiotic Loki still playing tricks on us." Chuckled Ullr. "Back to Jotunheim, Helheim and Asgard." The father joined in. They returned back to the village and had one final festival before going back to Norway. Hog roasts lit, vegetables chopped, dancers spinning almost floating like flames above firewood, horns blowing, lutes being plucked and flutes chirping all night long. Ullr was so delighted to have his father back.

As they travelled back to Norway they waved off England. "We've done a good job Ullr." The father exclaimed. "Indeed" Ullr synced. They reach Norway and settled for the night. "Was he bothering you?" a strange mysterious but soft voice echoed. "Who are you?" Ullr asked. "I am Odin, the king of all gods.

Thank you for killing Fenrir. He was a pain for us and definitely Tyr!" Odin spoke. "Ha, yes nice one Odin" Thor guffawed. "Wow you've always been there for me?" Ullr questioned. "You have deserved it son." His father tapped his shoulder that had a badge with Odin's eye on it. The gods hovered down from a strong beam of light breaking the night sky like a tear in paper and pressed three badges on his shoulder. One with Odin's eye for spotting his father's disappearance. The other with a thunder bolt on for striking hard and first and the last with an axe for the beauty of the blades and bravery. "When you perish you will come to my castle and be knighted, Ullr the god of snow and independent combat" Odin exclaimed...

Garug's Great Battle

by Jamie Wilkinson

With a fuzzy vision and the scent of fish filling the air, Garug awoke on the most important day of his life. As that day him and his army were going to take over London. He got up put on his armour, grabbed his battle-axe and wandered around his village. Garug bought his breakfast, ate it and then brought his army onto the boiling beach. He ordered them to get onto the long-ships and start preparing for battle. Once they were prepared they set sail for London.

Garug and his army waited patiently and bravely. Sea shanties were being sung and the waves were nowhere to be seen. They had sailed for a long time and had started to approach their destination. Everyone cheered ad Garug blew his Viking horn to let London know the Vikings were there. They got to the beach and began to fight. Everything was going superb for Garug until something happened.

They began to become outnumbered as most of his army were getting brutally slaughtered. Fire was in Garug's eyes as he went berserk to try and fight but it didn't work. Some of his army fled while the rest fought by Garug's side. They battled for around 30 minutes before everyone but Garug was dead. "What do I do now!" he mumbled to himself. Garug ran but found himself to be surrounded. The army of London closed in and knocked him out.

In a panicked state of mind, Garug woke up locked up somewhere. "Where am I?!" Garug bellowed … no answer. He waited for a response but didn't get one. He was enraged and tried to break down the steel bars keeping him in. He eventually gave up and just sat there. He fell asleep. All of a sudden, he got woken up by the sound of the cell door opening. "Who's there?" he asked. Unexpectedly, some of his army walked in and helped him up. "Did you think we would leave you to die," a fellow soldier said, "no way!" Garug was overjoyed. Him and his army ran out to the long-ship and set sail for Norway.

They celebrated all day and night. They were exhausted so rested. They woke up and kept on going. Suddenly, the ship stopped and jolted forward. The water turned an inky, midnight black and the crew became alarmed. "Get ready men because the Kraken is here!" Garug screamed. Tentacles rose from the water as the deadly beast screeched. Axes and swords were swung and arrows were shot in an attempt to kill it. It did nothing but make its head come out of the water. Garug got an idea.

He remembered that the Krakens weak spot was its beady eye. Knowing that he picked up a gleaming sword, jumped and stabbed it in it's big, fat, ugly eye. It squealed in pain and its tentacles drooped. It stopped moving. It was dead. Cheers rose from the now mobilised ship. Garug was pulled from the water feeling amazing as he had just killed the Kraken.

The ship started sailing back to Norway… again, while everyone partied…again. The had got back to Norway the next day. The whole village was relieved to know Garug was ok. He told everyone what happened and how he killed the Kraken. Hearing that, the King stepped down and made Garug the new king for   killing   the   one   and   only   Kraken.

Chris's Adventure

by Jayden Brachio

Chris woke up and stretched, with his hands in the air and left his room, with a beam on his face, he was ready for the day. He yelled for his parents and was alarmed because his parents didn't answer? He thought maybe they went outside so exited his house with odd thoughts. To his surprise he found some villagers sobbing, others with a frown. He instantly ran up to his parents, feeling muddled he asked his dad what was happening, he was dazed by the overwhelming news that his dad, whilst shedding a tear and wiping it from his face, clarified how the village leader was nowhere to be seen.

"W……… WHAT!" Chris, shouted irritated, "He's disappeared? W…what".

Chris ran into his house crying and then ran upstairs and grabbed his blade his dad gave him for his 8th birthday, he ran back outside to the middle of the village and shouted "Let's find him!".

"Are you sure Chris?" replied some of the people

"Positive!" bellowed Chris, in excitement.

"Ok, whatever you say" said Chris.

So they climbed into the long ship and proceeded to get ready for fighting the other Vikings with bow and arrows full and people with armour and swords.

"The ship still functioning Dad?" asked Chris.

"Yes son!" answered Dad.

"Weird how it's still in perfect condition it's been here for centuries!" replied Chris.

"Yeah very" said Dad.

Within minutes they set navigating.

The tornado was fierce; Vikings were being knocked around. Finally, they were flung out of the whirling winds!

After spinning for a while they finally stopped. Everyone was dizzy, the problem was that the boat was still moving.

"I'm tired!" whinged everyone on the ship.

"Me too!" exhaled Chris, as the stars began to lustre in the shadowy moonbeam.

Abruptly a Viking long ship appeared. We started to launch bow and arrows at them.

"You, over there, go over there and fire at them!" Chris instructed.

"OK chief!" the crew obeyed.

The longboat started to vibrate, like an earthquake, we thought how we needed to get vengeance for our leader.

"Now start fighting them horrific people!" said Chris furiously.

"Ok Chief!" said the crew, swiftly they vanished.

Everyone had a sigh of relief and others were uninterested from training all day. We were making sure nothing came from behind us.

"Where even is he?" tiredly said Chris,

We heard a really loud noise in the distance in the ocean and we went silent for a brief minute. The sound stops so we thought we were fine. Suddenly a ghost monster began to attack our boat, we all panicked and ran to the cannons and to pick up our bow and arrows. We started to shoot at the monster but our weapons did not damage it. We kept on fighting then suddenly our ship was launched into the air. We were screaming and then unexpectedly everything went black…

All of the crew woke up on a piece of land with a village in the distance, they were in a lot of pain, but none of them could remember how they got there. They decided to go to the village to see if they would let them in and see if they had their leader. They all walked for hours arriving to ask if they knew about their missing leader and described what he looked like. They said they didn't know. But in the distance they heard "HELP ME", repeated again and again.

They followed the voice and found their leader locked inside a cage!

"Let me out, look under that rock, the key is hidden there" the leader screamed in anger.

"Thank you" whispered the leader.

"We saved you, thank god, let's get out of here and find home" uttered Chris.

They sprinted out of the village without looking back.

Hours later they arrived home, the villagers were shouting "We're so glad to have you back leader".

"You're a hero Chris" said the leader.

"You saved my life, I can't repay you for the kindness you have shown, I will give you this medal for being amazing".

Everyone started cheering and throwing Chris in the air. His parents launched confetti on him and he loved it and was feeling like a hero.

"Let's have a party to celebrate" happily said the leader.

"YAY" Chris said excitedly, as he walked like a hero with a smile on his face.

"WOOOooo!" everyone was cheering. All were enjoying the music at the party. Lots were dancing, then came an announcement…

"We have a special guest and that's CHRIS!" the leader declared, everyone was applauding.

"This is the face of a true hero, let's party with him".

"This is the best day ever" said Chris, as his mum and dad lifted him up and danced with him.

The leader revealed "You are now declared a warrior   Viking".

Archeus' Adventure

by Jiah Parkes

With his head feeling heavy, Archeus awoke with nightmares swarming his brain like a virus on a computer. The sounds of trees being chopped down was normal to him but this time was different- his dad, Kratos, was gathering wood for Archeus' mother's cremation. Before that, Archeus had been out to hunt, he was a very good and accurate archer, his bow was crafted by his mother, Faye. He headed out again to find something to feast on - his dad said the forests near home are great for food. Suddenly a deer had appeared and Archeus reached for the bow and took a shot at the wild creature. It dropped dead with blood pouring from its skin Archeus stood up and celebrated, bringing the deer back home.

'' DAD I HAVE FOOD!'' screamed Archeus at the top of his lungs. ''Cook it boy, then we can eat.'' exclaimed Kratos with tears rolling down his cheeks.

Archeus knew if he said anything about Faye he'd make his dad even more sad. Archeus stood up and grabbed the axe and offered it to Kratos. ''Come on let's….''

Archeus stuttered and dropped Leviathan. His dad was frozen. His jaw dropped and he knew what he'd done. The only person he could trust now was uncle Vic. He'd taken off using the power of the axe and plummeted into the snow.

''Uncle! Father is frozen what shall I do?'' asked Archeu stressed.

Vic was ashamed of his nephew.

''Where's Faye?'' he questioned Archeus.

The boys heart sank.

''Dead.'' Mumbled Archeus.

''No she isn't, ''Vic answered.

''Well you can't be a lonely child, you need to go to an island far out at sea, if you want your father back, go now!'' demanded Uncle Vic.

Two hours had past and Archeus arrived at Kratos' boat and realised a gang of men were standing outside of it.

"Look it's a shooting star!'' screamed Aspen.

''Don't be stupid, it's the middle of the day.'' exclaimed Endor, correcting his friend.

''AHHH!''

Archeus hit the ground like a bolt of lightning, he saw the men running back to the boat to armour up.

''I'll be taking this.'' Archeus cackled.

''Not so fast boy.'' The men answered.

Oh no, he had to kill them men quick. He froze Aspen's foot to the ship and threw Endor off the deck.

''Spare me please.'' Endor pleaded.

Archeus hated killing people with a passion so with those words spoken to his face he let him go.

Thirty minutes passed, the young twelve-year-old had never been so frightened and alone. He believed Lord Odin would find and banish him, he'd lost his mother and maybe even his dad, for some time he thought he might lose himself.

* Kraken noises* ?

Sixteen massive tentacles reached up and attached to the boat and lifted its wet maroon body and googly yellow eyes. Its skin was sodden and water poured down its face. It ripped holes in the boat filling it with aquamarine salty water and pulled it down to the sea bed, Archeus had to act fast, first with its legs, then next its head. SLICE!

The limbs of the creature spewed with lime green blood and it couldn't control its body. Archeus threw the axe through its head and it dived back in the blood infested water. The boy beckoned with excitement, he was a true warrior.

He'd been sailing for hours now and still hadn't found the island. ''Mother I've failed you, I can't do this!'' he screamed kicking at his father's axe.

All hope was lost until a beam of light shone down on a rocky molten island. He jumped with joy and a smile formed on his face. He leapt out of the rusted wooden boat and darted right to the cave. The volcanic explosions continued and as he entered the small gap a crack of lightning crashed through the roof.

''You are coming with me, as well as the Ancient Flames.'' ?

''Leave me alone you evil man.'' ?

''I'm Thor, god of thunder, son of Odin, I take orders from no one!''

Archeus used the pillars and cut them down to make the temple unstable. ZAP! The boy was knocked down to the floor, he quickly dodged the flying hammer and froze it to the wall. He proceeded to glue Thor's legs to the floor making him unable to move. The boy had obtained both the hammer and the flames.

Archeus' heart thumped rapidly like a World War II machine gun. He dashed through the sky using the power of the hammer - he was so fast the trees tore his skin apart. Somehow he couldn't feel it, that didn't bother him though, his childhood hero was Thor now he could be just like him. Aside from that his father was still in the ice and it only lasted for a day, he needed to move fast.

Archeus was so elated about defeating Thor, god of thunder, and presenting the gift of the Mjnor hammer to Kratos but he needed to get home fast. As he entered the wooden cabin he knew his mother kept a ritual book inside but where was it?

Come on Archeus think. He thought to himself.

''Under the bear skin!'' a muffled voice said behind him.

He tore the skin apart leaving him with the book. He grabbed it, the flames and the axe starting the ritual allowing father to leave.

ritual sounds ?

panting x4 ?

Archeus was so full of emotions all his words came out at once.

''I have some explaining to do father....''

Bill's Adventure

by Josh Watson

Half asleep, Bill huddled with his sheepskin, the
sound of people spluttering and coughing made him
confused and he questioned what the sounds were?
He went to check it out. "Come on Bill!" shouted
Dave. Bodies were running everywhere getting
shields and axes. Bills' bossy dad, like always,
bossing everyone about, telling them what they can
and can't do in this village. Bill with his messy hair
and buzzing flies all around him. Bill felt like he was
nothing in this village, he felt useless.

As Bill slowly opened the door, he saw that the
Saxons had kidnapped his mother and that was why
everyone was panicking and shouting, but at that
moment Bill stepped into his proper Viking shoes and
shouted "Save my mum!" he felt happy with himself.
They took food, shields and swords, chucked them in
the ships carelessly, they equipped themselves with
armour and packed everything. They knew this will
take days but Bill thought it would take as long as it
would take. Bill and his father jumped into the boat
with a thump. There were loads of Viking villagers in
it and they screamed fiercely, "set sail".

A 11-year-old and a 40-year-old going to save
their mum and wife. No turning back now.

As they took off with a flash, Bill looked into the
distance, "Look at that?" questioned Bill, "Is that a
shark or a whale, what is it dad?" asked Bill, "The

creature I've been hunting for years" answered Dave. Angrily they fired arrows at it, whistling in the wind like bombs dropping from the sky, it moaned in pain, it's pitch red eyes matching its scaly skin and jagged teeth, it roared so loud it pushed back the boats a little. Then the ferocious creature shot a spike at the boat and hit dad "nooo!" cried Bill. Bill shot an arrow back right into its eye, it fell back into the water with a massive splash, "dad?" murmured Bill, "Keep on going son", explained Dave. "Bill throw me into the ocean", his father said. As Bill chucked his father into the ocean he felt heartbroken. They carried on sailing but a few sailing minutes later they felt some drops of rain, "Oh No" shouted Bill.

As they felt cold drops of cold rain, the Viking crew were all asleep, except from uncle Barry. [The leader for now] "Look, a tornado!" shouted Barry, "Everyone awake" screeched Bill "take cover" he shrieked. The wind was shaking the boat, parts of their village was in the tornado, they were all worried but they didn't give up. Whistling surrounded them crack, crack, crack went the hail, splash, splash, splash went the rain, the tornado left the area after hours. They saw the island with Bill's mother on it. She had seen people flying off the boat in that tornado and wind. "We made it!" cried Bill, "Woohoo" shouted Uncle Barry.

As they were munching on meat in their blankets they saw some Saxon ships heading towards them, "Come on, not again!" shouted Bill, "Get ready", Bill said with power.

Canons being fired, Anglo-Saxon ships being destroyed and only 4 ships to go, then at that moment the Anglo-Saxon ships shot 3 canons right at one of Bills boats and Bang! Bills ships were down to two. Bill loads up a fireball and fires right at their boats, destroys the third and second ship only one to go, Bills boat beside him get destroyed, they both charge inwards to each other, "Yaa" the Vikings shouted, everyone fighting, all that could be heard are the clinks of the swords making a connection. Bill finished them off. But whilst Bill was sneaking in the Anglo-Saxon leader said, "We shall kill the leaders' wife!". Bill jumped in and killed the Saxons, then he untied his sad mum, then returned back to the ship and started to sail back to their village.

Bill felt heroic and powerful, his mum felt blessed. Bill was explaining what happened, he told her that they killed the sea creature but sadly Dave passed away, "Wait, noooo!" shouted Bills mother, "How?". "Well he got shot with a spike from the sea creature right into the chest. This is where we defeated the sea creature. We then passed a massive tornado, then defeated the Saxon ships.

Then a familiar voice said, "Hi son, hi wife", it was Dave! "Your alive" shouted Bill.

As the boat hits shore people in the village welcome them back.

"THIS IS TO BILL" shouted Dave, "Woohoo" screamed all the dirty Vikings," he did not give up, he battled on, he saved my beautiful Britney, he saved every single one of you!". "Let's dig in" spluttered Dave, there was crunching, munching and slurping, as they made their way through: steak, pork, chicken and vegetable soup. Bill said "Well done Vikings for helping me and my family, including my amazing

Uncle Barry, for comforting me throughout that massive Viking trip". As the moon rose there was dancing, talking and happiness surrounding the village.

Vic's Viking Adventure

by Joshua Burley

In the middle of the deep blue sea Viking long ships clashed exchanging blows. Vic lost his balance quickly on the deck. He stumbled to the deck and grazed his pale face. Vic's mother spoke kind words to him to check that he was ok. Vic wasn't like other Vikings, he was wimpier and he was an embarrassment to his father. Vic's father was the chief of the Viking village. He was muscular and scary, everything Vic wasn't!

Halvar [Vic's dad] climbs slowly up the dragon head and faced his audience to announce that he had stolen a magic sword from his sworn enemy, that turns everything to gold.

Proudly Halvar is swinging the magic sword around when from the tip of the golden blade out shot a beam of gold! The shinning beam pierced through a member of the crowd. Halvar did not realise it was his wife Malbec. In the crowd some stood in silence while others screamed as Malbec turned to gold.

So as Vic looked around he realised his mum was a golden statue. His sister Hella had covered her face with her hands, as tears streamed down her face.

Halvar knew the only way to return Malbec to normal was to go to Mau Mau island to destroy the sword in the volcano. Vic shouted "I'll take the quest and return mum to normal".

Vic decided to leave next sundown so as not be seen by enemies. Setting sail across the star lit ocean it was quite peaceful. As the sun rose Vic and his crew [which consisted of his father, his sister and various other Vikings] see a Viking long ship coming up over the horizon. The enemy armed themselves with swords, axes and long bows, Vic's team did the same. A battle ensued Halvar brought only his best warriors and even brought the golden sword. Despite being heavily out-numbered Halvar and his men were putting up a fight even turning some of them to gold. After the battle was over Halvar and his men were victorious.

As they continued to sail the waves got stronger and the wind picked up, they saw a tornado on a rampage ripping trees off nearby islands. Vic yelled "Turn around ", but it was too late they were being sucked into the tornado.

"Grab onto something" shouted Halvar.

The tornado was fierce Vikings were being knocked around, finally they were flung out of the tornado.

After spinning for a while they finally stopped, everyone was dizzy, the problem was that the boat was still moving. No one was aware of that until Hella warned," Brace for impact ".

When Vic awoke he saw his entire crew unconscious along with the wreckage of the ship, it was completely destroyed.

When the crew awoke Vic was just sitting on a rock looking out into the horizon.

"Maybe there's still a way to get to Mau Mau island "said Hella.

"It's worth a shot "added Halvar.

"Maybe we can "responded Vic.

"We could us the planks from the wreckage to build the deck and use our clothes for sails, "added Vic.

"That could work "responded Halvar.

"Then let's get to it "exclaimed vic.

While Halvar and the Viking soldiers built the deck and the mast, Hella was sewing together the Vikings clothes because she had experiences sewing. Two days until summer solstice but they still had a long way to go.

The remainder of the journey was smooth. Once they reached Mau Mau island and began walking up the volcano, across the ravine and up to the volcanos crater.

"Vic you got us here, you get the honour of destroying the sword" remarked Halvar.

Vic threw the sword into the lava, the volcano starting erupting, everyone ran as fast as they could back down the volcano and across the ravine, but as Vic crossed the middle of the ravine, the walkway broke, Vic had to take a leap of faith, he jumped, he didn't make it, Vic closed his eyes and expected it, but he didn't feel himself falling. He looked up and saw Halvar and Hella pulling him up.

"You're the bravest Viking ever Vic" remarked his   father.

Hallie and Hettie's Adventure

by Lexi Hill

With a blurred vision and sense of confusion, Hallie and her sister Hettie awoke to the sound of shouting that echoed within the village. Hastily she leapt out of bed and stormed over to the window. Within a blink of an eye she stood still as a stern soldier waiting for battle. Hettie laid in bed huddled into her sheepskin blanket not knowing what had happened.

"Wake up" shouted Hallie.

Then suddenly they ran as fast as lightening pushing open their mums' bedroom door.

Their eyes filled up with fear as they trembled through the empty room wondering where their mum disappeared to. They walked outside and saw a crowd of sweaty Vikings surrounding them, slowly a thin piece of paper laid on the floor with the symbol of a shield from the evil Viking, Vik and his crew! Hallie picked it up and read it.

"One thousand pieces of gold and jewellery must be handed to me within 4 days and I will give you what you came for."

She read the note and dropped it to the floor in shock, without warning Hettie untied the rope connecting to a Viking longboat.

"Come on", she shouted.

"We don't need gold and jewellery to save mum".

They hopped on the boat and sailed off to sea.

Rumbling and crackling in the dark dull distance clouds began to grow and thunder began to roar. As the waves grew bigger the Viking longboat began to motion faster.

"What's happening?" questioned Hallie, gulping with terror.

"Pull the rope", barked Hettie.

The sails grew stronger, the thunder and lightning suddenly started to disappear like magic. So they set off with bravery shivering down their spine.

With a mother missing, the two girls sailed along the calm sea. Vik's followers were approaching them.

"What's that", asked Hallie.

Hettie looked into the distance and saw the pattern of a shield on the side of a boat, it was getting closer and closer. A bomb shoots with an extremely good aim.

"Shoot that thing!", exclaimed Hettie.

A bomb shot and the enemies turned around and scattered.

Stranded out at sea, feeling tired, they steered the longboat as the wavy water rippled. Without a warning the waves were stringer and the boat began to fill with water, as puddles appeared on the wooden planks. Hallie looked overboard and saw that they were going to be swept underwater. Hettie grabbed her hand and they jumped. Catching their breath, they hung onto the floating wooden planks. She shielded her eyes from the blinding sun and looked around for Vik's island. Time dragged past but with eagle eyes she saw the small green island, so they started to paddle to land.

Arriving on the island, they pulled themselves up against the soft yellow sand. Feeling heroic they wandered the island quietly not to be caught. In the corner of their eye they spotted a dark gloomy cave. As they walked inside they find a door, Hettie pushes the door and it creaks open. She took a peep inside and looked left and right. Finally, they found their mum, tied up against the pointy rocks. Out of nowhere footsteps echoed in the long distance. They weren't just anyone's footsteps; it was Vik the evil Vikings. They crept back into the shadows

"Who's there?", bellowed Vik.

Brave Hettie stepped forward, shielding her mum and sister behind her.

"Ugh it's you", he mumbled.

"Have you bought me my treasure?"

"No, but I found this" Hettie exclaimed, as she reached with her thin hand into her pocket.

She grabbed the most beautiful shiny piece of jewellery she had ever found. (She had found this as they searched the island earlier) Vik's eyes lit up with amazement.

"Give me that", Vik demanded.

"Give us peace then" whispered Hallie.

They declared peace and promised to never harm anyone again.

Later that day, sailing in silence, feeling proud and courageous, they returned home, with their hearts pounding out of their chests with excitement. They could hear the loud drums beating overhead and music being played by the villagers, welcoming them. The two sisters explained to the village how they came to make harmony and Vik's promise of peace.

No-one else will be harmed. At the end of the day everyone had a feast to celebrate their success of bringing home their mum. They danced and pranced to the music. While their mum perched resting her tired legs, listening to the laughter of happiness.

June and Bob's Viking Adventure!

by Mollie Basson

Curiously looking ahead like nosy ferrets, June and Bob could smell the salty, clear sea swimming up their delicate nostrils. The adventurous girl and caring boy, could feel the fresh, cold air as it gently touched their rosy cheeks. Silently, the children felt the choppy, energetic water bobbing up and down, under their small feet. They could hear the crystal ocean rippling as it got stronger and stronger! Bob, (who was June's best friend,) is only eleven and June was twelve! The two children were going for an exciting ride on their new Viking Longboat!

"June, where are you taking us to?" asked Bob curiously.

"You will see!" answered June in a squeaky tone.

The seas grew stronger and stronger as time went past, and at one point the boat nearly tipped over!

"Ahhh!" screamed Bob, starting to get worried now!

"Haha!" whispered June to herself, loving the stomach turning ride! Where are they going, are they safe?

Suddenly, June came to an abrupt halt. Bob was feeling all sorts of emotions, like a huge rollercoaster whizzing round and round – worried, unsure, confused and sick!

"June, where are we, why are we in the middle of seas?" asked Bob frantically, his eyebrows turning into confusion.

"We are going for a swim, Bob!" June blurted out.

Bob's mother had given the two children the village necklace to keep safe for the week!

"Remember June, we have got the necklace now on the boat!" answered Bob in a worried tone.

"Off we go!" muttered June, ignoring Bob plugging her ears!

Bob and June went out to sea to swim and because June ignored Bob, she had totally gone mad and completely forgot. Bob and June hadn't realised! A moment later, on an island with greedy, stealing vikings, one king viking, cheekily came along and stole the precious, valuable necklace!

Now, June and Bob were far out sea and couldn't see their boat! Bob forgot about the necklace too! What were the children going to do? When would they come back to the boat?

With charcoal, smoke filled clouds approaching aggressively above, June and Bob sat silently on a smooth, cold rock. Suddenly, an almighty storm struck and the two children agreed they should go back to the boat. But they waited for a few minutes for the rumbling storm to stop! When it did, the determined children finally swam slowly back. Just at that moment, as they were silently swimming, June heard terrible thunder!

"Bob, Bob!" shouted June at the top of her squeaky voice!

Bob knew what was going on! The two frightened people, bobbed their heads slowly out of the water and looked up at the beastly, ear-piercing, deafening storm. As quick as lightning, the children got back to swimming and tried as mighty and furiously as possible to make it back to the boat calmly and safely!

"Stay next to me June!" bellowed Bob, nervously!

"We can make it Bob, we're brave and strong!" added June in a hopeful, trembling shaky voice!

Will they make it back safely?

Nearly making it back to the boat, June and Bob swam determined to stay together. Pounding aggressively, Junes heart fell out of her chest. Suddenly, out of the corner of the children's eyes, they luckily saw their Viking longboat!

"Wait a second," cried Bob gasping for breath.

"Nooo!" he screamed,

"The boat is sinking quick we need to save it now!" he bellowed.

June and Bob rushed petrified! As they got back to the destroyed boat, luckily June found the circle gap of glass loose and that was what was letting the water float in! With the water gushing in, luckily with the teamwork of June and Bob, they managed to find a same shaped piece of glass that fitted, unbelievably perfectly into the unpleasant gap!

"Teamwork makes the dream work!" yelled them both together in tune!

"Now, we should get on the boat!" said Bob.

"Nooo, Bob this can't be true, the village necklace has gone!" screamed June,

"We will never be trusted again!" exclaimed Bob.

"I know exactly where and who done this, Bob follow me, I will lead you there, jump on!" whispered June!

Does June know for certain?

Starring at each other silently, they could hear the sea flowing and rippling gracefully. Their eyes growing huger and huger as they started bulging out of both their heads!

"Bob, you can trust me, let's do this, yeah?!" shouted June in a cowboy voice.

Suddenly, Bob's eyes started whirling round and round like a washing machine, and then all of a sudden he fell to the floor of the boat! "Bob, no, come on wake up don't faint on me!" muttered June her hands shaking.

"Right, I guess I am on my own fighting the Vikings then." mumbled the frightened, unsure girl.

June started to slowly ride the boat to the side of the blue sea, in the shade of the hanging trees at the edge of an island. Then, she made sure no one was watching and very carefully, June carried Bob. Whilst lifting up a little square latch, that that led to the underneath of the boat. There was a little room and one bed. June lay Bob down caringly on the bed. A tear ran down her cold, pale cheeks.

"I am going to be so scared here without you Bob, can I do this on my own?" the girl questioned out loud to herself. June was worried and frightened that she couldn't face the Vikings on her own. What was she going to do?...

Looking at Bob, hopeful that he would wake up, June climbed up the crooked, steep stairs. Her head popped up and at that moment June could see out the very corner of her eye the Island of Greedy Vikings coming her way! Her heart was pounding and her cheeks were no longer dripping with tears, they were dripping with sweat! June was awfully tired.

"I am exhausted, but I know I can win this necklace back!" June said. "Hold back in there, Bob! "shouted June even though she knew he hadn't woken up.

The seas crashed, the wind grew stronger again and the start of the fight began!

"Come on JB you can do this!" shouted June.

JB was the name of their boat! [J for June and B for Bob!]

"I have never been more ready for this fight!" said June ready as ever, her eyes concentrating so hard her eyes looked like they were going to pop out any second!

As the Vikings came closer one fat one yelled, "And the fight begins!.."

Huddling and carefully forming together, the clouds grew white and then said something – Go June – it said high above overlooking the two Longboats. The Viking Longboats crashed and boomed loudly together, as June could see the village necklace hanging in the grubby Vikings hand. Suddenly, the enemies boat all of a sudden broke and started to fall slowly apart! June was in luck! The selfish, Vikings gave up and finally threw the necklace to June!

"Yay, you rude Vikings will get payback one day!" screeched June. Then, in the blink of an eye, the other Viking Longboat disappeared! June ran down to Bob as fast as she could and when she looked at the bed… Bob was awake!!

"Oh yay, Bob you're awake!" shouted June!

"I won the necklace back Bob!" screamed June, jumping in joy.

"That is fantastic June, Wow, I can't believe you done it! Anyway, we probably should get back home now, it has been a long day for the two of us, on our overwhelming adventure!" said Bob quietly.

Once the two children had made it home, they told their mum, [Bobs mum, Junes Bobs friend but June calls her mum anyway,] what had happened. Luckily, their mum had said to trust them whatever happened!

"Right, let's go and celebrate that you got the necklace now, with a delicious and the best roast dinner ever!" shouted mum joyfully! "Yay!" they both screamed joyfully. They all went to party and celebrate.

"This has been an adventure!" muttered June.

"Don't worry, at least you are safe and happy at home." said mum. The Viking family all had a huge smile on their face and the sun came out and beamed down on them. Their eyes twinkled as they danced happily after their amazing victory! The Viking family all danced together. June and Bob were rewarded top Vikings in the village because of all the protection they showed to this village!

"We can do anything!" cheered the children.

Mia of Atlanta's Adventure

by Niamh Courtney

The festival of lights made people dance joyfully in the moon lit sky. The night sky was surrounded with the laughs of men and women. Roasted delights were cooking on the fire. The heat from the fire pit licked their skin.

Out of nowhere, the old wrinkled chief sent Mia, who was perched on the edge of a sycamore tree bench next to the chief, to his flamboyantly dressed hut to bring him a sheep skin blanket for his cold peely skin. After a few minutes in chief Asfants room she found a spotless white sheepskin quilt. Returning to the festival she laid it gently on his rough shoulders just like he requested. As the festival came to its end Frayer [chief Asfants daughter] got her tired father prepared for his 7-hour slumber, when she notices a particular diamond called the Safire's Heart wasn't in her father's display case, it wasn't anywhere.

With fear in her eyes Mia ran towards the rundown harbour. Panicked, she climbed aboard a small longboat. Untying the fisherman's knot she drifted off to the dark night. The last thing she saw from the village was pitchforks and fire until a blanket of mist covered it all. Now her home was a distant memory.

Early the next morning, Asfant declared "We will search high and low for this underserving criminal I promise you your revenge on her gloomy soul."

Preparing their largest two boats Chief Asfant and his army of soldiers set on their mission. Several minutes later, a sharp breeze came alongside a tribe of angry storm clouds. A percentage of Chief Asfants fighters complained of hearing crackles of thunder getting closer and closer and louder and louder. BANG! Thunder hit the boat. Floating defencelessly in the water Frayers boat was sinking. "Help" "Let us into your boat" "Today please", she shouted in a sarcastic voice because they were taking so long.

"After recovering every lazy unreliable soldier from the depths of the sea, we are off ".

A few hours later barrels of survival equipment were rolling side to side on the ship, men and women were sliding side to side on their rowing benches. Leaning over the edge of the poorly constructed ship Asfant realised rapids surrounded them in every direction imaginably. Hitting the the side of the boat on cliffs and rocks scraping and scratching onto the boat. Scraachhherr. The army of people had been knocked into the complete wrong direction.

Sailing on their terrifying journey, unaware of where they were, a dark mist covered their view. With the boat undirected of where it was heading, the ship started to wobble. Minutes later, the fog cleared its path, revealing enemy ships closing in on them. Ready to fight Malacrat (Leader of enemy army) and her men leapt onto Asfants boat, unprepared he bellowed "Charge!" at his revolting crew. Malacrat had underestimated Asfants laughing stock of a group. Chief Asfants team had won the most dangerous battle in 126 years with Asfant in charge.

Persisting on their tedious quest for revenge, Salapac (The most arrogant crew member) saw a glimpse of a shiny, red diamond. Reaching out from Asfants pocket. Seconds later, Frayer caught him red handed holding the Safiers Heart. Salapac was thrown from the edge of the boat to defend for himself. A few days later they hit a rogue island and noticed a boat had Asfants emblem, so they went to investigate. ZZzzzz. With the sound of that they rushed in. Desperate for forgiveness Chief Asfant ordered his men to gently tip-toe into the small cramped ship to discover Mia asleep on a rusty, dusty bed in the bottom of the boat.

After various smooth and steady trip days, back to Attana (Their village) Mia finally woke up with her family surrounding her. A few months later, the village threw a party that lasted for weeks.

That's the story of Mia of Attana!

Aiden's Adventure

by Olivia Farris

As a sweet aroma wafted up his nose, Aiden partied with his family, creaking the charred wooden floor boards as they threw each other round and round the room. Glasses raised as hot sweaty men cheered celebrating the official first day of summer. Babies cried whilst up-beat music blared and stamping feet danced the night away. Aiden could see that everyone was enjoying themselves so much so nobody wanted the dazzling day to come to an end. He knelt down and stroked the furry sheep skin that lay underneath his feet as he pondered over tomorrows adventure lurking upon him. Suddenly there was a high pitched screech that sounded as if there was a ship arriving in the harbour.

"What was that siren?" screamed Aiden, trying to be heard over the deafening music

"That wasn't a siren son, that was just the beat of the song!" replied his father as he joined the conga line that was wrapping around the room as if it were a snake.

"Oh, ok!" shouted the boy, as he reached for his father's shoulders.

Suddenly, out of nowhere, the whole village plunged into darkness alerting the Vikings at once. Striking their swords out of their leather trousers, all men became straight faced and winced trying to take a glimpse of what was happening. Just then the lights came back on and to everyone disbelief, but the chief's, nothing had happened. Aiden knew something was out of the ordinary but he just couldn't put his finger on it; or could he. Everyone realised that the day was almost over so they packed up their helmets, swords and shields and began to walk out of the creaky hinged door. All was well till a blood curdling scream echoed around the village.

"Dad!" yelled Aiden, as he burst out the door and into the cold gentle breeze.

"He's been kidnapped!" everyone yelled in unison, as they hurled themselves onto a nearby ship ready to set sail on the ripping tidal waves.

Aiden had already packed for this mission and in his bag was: a net, a rope, a sandwich (of course) and a water bottle fresh from the nearby river.

As the ship set sail, thunder clouds erupted filling all spirits with doom. All cheers were dulled down and everyone became silent; all apart from Aiden who was raring to go. It wasn't long till rain began to pour and start to flood the boat.

"All hands on deck!" screamed the vice chief (Olaf) as the water levels rose upon them, filling the ship with buckets and buckets of salty rainwater.

Ear-deafening thunder also arrived, as hot sweaty men heaved crates upon the old crooked deck to try and filter the water out of the boat. Suddenly, it became too much for the very little amount of men and the boat was being weighed down like an anchor so much so that it began to sink. Yells of horror rose upon the crowd as they no longer had a boat and had to swim to get to safety.

The waves were as if they were fighting each other now and Aiden and his crewmates were not very excited at all to have to swim, but as they had trained in the shallow waters of the harbour they were advanced swimmers; making it ever so easy for them. They could almost glide through the water but at this very moment the furious storm was not helping. Aiden wasn't as good a swimmer as all the grown-ups but had learnt a trick or few from his father's training lessons and soon got the hang of it. Just then, Aiden felt an enormous creature like thing swoop under his grubby elongated toe nails which sent a shiver down his spine. There is a beast in the water! "Ahhh!" screamed Aiden as he squirmed around and tried to leap onto Olaf's back.

"Oy, get off of me, you beastly boy," yelled the man. "What on earth has gotten into you?"

"There...there," screamed the boy.

"There what?" replied the man.

"There's a creature, no, no, not a creature a beast... a brain boggling beast!" screeched the boy.

Everyone had heard Olaf and Aiden's conversation and were now so freaked out that they started frantically throwing their arms and legs in the air and screaming at the top of their lungs.

"Help!" squealed a small boy, no older than Aiden.

"Everyone calm down; we are going to be fine." explained Olaf trying to hold back his fright.

As his heart pounded, Aiden breathed a sigh of relief after noticing the monstrosity of a monster has finally vanished and moved onto a tastier and fresh smelling meal. Cheers wailed around the gloomy grey sky; but not for long! Humongous waves crashed along the men ruining their rhythm. Land was needed and fast! Terror reigned upon the crew as they began to give up.

"Come on lads we can't give up especially not now, look how far we have come!" somehow Aiden's words lifted the spirits of the worn out drenched men (who were back on track and ready for the rest of theirquest).

All of a sudden, a glimpse of land shone in the corner of Olaf's eyes. "Land ahoy!" he yelled and as soon as all the crew heard his cry they picked up the pace of their swimming and started to also see the huge red flag of the enemy's land. Nobody cheered as they knew from past experience that all is not done and the quest is not yet finished. In no time they arrived at the familiar looking island and through a huge doorway, they could see Victor tied up and struggling to breathe, as tape covered his beard, which was a bird's nest and may even have some eggs in there too.

"Come on lads," whispered Olaf

"We can do this!".

Carefully, all the crew crept up to the long house quietly as they could and began to untie the poor leader, all whilst the residents of the enemy's island were still celebrating summer solstice. Eventually, Victor had been untied and immediately leant against the crowdsearching for his son.

"Aiden?" he screamed.

"Over here dad," murmured a distant voice.,

"I have found our getaway plan!".

He was in a newly-polished boat in the harbour of the other tribe's land ready to set sail on the choppy sea.

On the way back from the island, the weather had calmed down and you could almost see the moon again. All of the crew could not hold back their excitement any more so they wailed and cheered throwing Aiden up in the air as his bravery had saved their land and its protector. Soon enough, the Vikings returned to their own island and threw their partners up in the air, celebrating their victory. Beers were chucked around and clunked together and all was well as they decided to carry the party on till the next morning. After the long day Aiden went to bed, his shoulders pushed back as he sat as tall as he could on his bearskin robe and dreamt of the next day's adventure ready to unfold into his very own hands.

Stormcloud's Adventure

by Olivia Martinez

On the beach Thunderclap and Stormcloud were digging in the sand when something caught Thunderclap's eye, it was a glimmering golden sphere! She tapped Stormcloud's shoulder immediately. Stormcloud was so bewildered of what she had just seen, it looked like ancient Viking treasure! Thunderclap was about to pick it up when Stormcloud screamed at her "NO don't touch it; it could be dangerous!". Thunderclap looked at her like she was crazy.

"Dangerous, really Stormy, ha, I laugh in the face of danger!" Thunderclap did her evil laugh, picked it up and disappeared into thin air.

Stormcloud got brain washed whilst Thunderclap was busy disappearing which means she now has no clue who Thunderclap is. She checked her watch and walked home from the beach like everything was fine. She was supposed to stay at Thunderclap's house tonight, but of course she had no memory of her so she walked home.

"Oh hi Stormy, I thought that you were staying the night at Thunderclap's." stuttered her mother.

Stormcloud was really confused!

"Who in the world is Thunderclap!" she exclaimed in confusion.

Her mother was standing there in shock; how could she forget her best friend!

"Right we are going to find her right now, Barry come here!" demanded her mum.

Her husband came charging down the stairs.

"Are you ok, what happened, oh hi sweetheart, aren't you supposed to be at Thunderclaps place?" said dad.

"No time to talk get on the long boat." shouted her mother.

And they were off, ready to save Thunderclap.

Stormcloud and her parents were sitting down until they got unsettled by another Viking long-ship arose from the thick mist. "Stormy get down NOW!" her mother screamed.

She did what she was told. An epic longship battle commenced, and after hours of fighting Stormcloud's parents won fair and square.

When the enemy ship left a massive storm came in.

"Ugh here we go again! screamed Stormcloud in anger.

"Stormy there is a hidden cabinet over there, go in and stay inside!" shouted her mother.

Stormcloud bolted to the cabinet and locked herself in. She was struggling to breathe, so she screamed. Her mother heard her cries, she broke down the door, picked up Stormcloud and jumped off the boat, her husband trailing behind her. The three of them started to swim quickly to a nearby island, coughing and spluttering all the way there. As soon as they reached the island they laid on the sand like beached whales, but realised where they were, Enemy island.

As soon as Stormcloud knew where she was she scrambled up to her feet and looked around.

"Mum, dad, look we are on the enemy's island" said Stormcloud in shock.

When they heard that they got up immediately.

"Wow look how many huts there are!" exclaimed Stormcloud in amazement.

They heard muffled cries coming from one of the huts, and started to get concerned. They walked towards the hut slowly, they heard the voice again, but it called "Stormy, in here".

Stormcloud recognised the voice instantly, it was Thunderclap. Stormcloud karate kicked the door down and saw Thunderclap tied to a chair. The enemies had cut off her long blond hair and made it short.

"Here let me help you" said Stormcloud.

She untied Thunderclap and gave her a hug.

"What did you do to your hair?" exclaimed Stormcloud.

"Oh the enemy cut it off, it's ok, it doesn't get in my face anymore".

Stormcloud was shocked she always talked about her long blond hair, and how much she loved it!

"Well, I think you've had a long day, let's go home, there's a feast waiting for us!" Stormcloud said.

"Yay alright, I am pretty hungry" replied Thunderclap.

"Come on you two chatterboxes, there's a feast waiting for us!" exclaimed Stormcloud parents.

Stormcloud and Thunderclap laughed and walked back to the long-ship holding hands.

When they got back, everyone cheered and celebrated Thunderclaps arrival. They ate the feast with joy and happiness inside of them.

Roberto's Adventure

by Toby Marsden

The young boy awoke to violent screaming and cries for help, something was happening, but what? He could taste the bitterness of fresh blood in the air, he hastily jumped out of bed and what he saw was indescribable. Lifeless bodies, slayed scattered around the ravaged village, it was a horrific sight for the boy, only sixteen, yet still having to face these disturbing events. Something could be heard very faintly, then something clicked it was the village leader.

Instantly Roberto darted out of his burnt house and through the charred ruins of the destroyed huts, he tried to keep up with the fearless warriors, but they were too well fitted for the Norwegian landscape.

"Nooooo", Roberto bellowed.

He had lost them and now was stranded in the cold climate of Norway. He was surrounded by miles of frosty wasteland, so his only choice was to push on trying to find the village leader.

As Roberto slowly walked on and on through miles of dull white fields he wondered to himself, will I ever find the village leader, will I ever get revenge on these cruel people? But as he was going to start another long session of talking to himself he heard a monstrous roar that echoed through the nearby valleys, scaring any wildlife close enough to hear it. Suddenly a horrific scent filled the air and a ten-foot beast stepped out of the shadowed surroundings, it swung its gigantic club. As Roberto dodged it he knew he couldn't fight this one, so he ran and hid, he was safe for now, but not for long.

Slowly but surely he pulled himself up from behind the rock scanning the area for enemy dangers, luckily the coast was clear so he made his move, he swiftly moved through the tall grass still being cautious because the wilderness is full creatures that can kill a man, well that's the case in Norway. As the boy moved on he came to a gate, a very highly protected gate, it was riddled with complex contraptions it was nearly impossible to breach, the only way to get in was the gate keepers.

"Please sir, I need to be seeing someone" Roberto begged.

"No" the gate keepers shouted.

There was no hope, so Robert tracked off into the wilderness once again to rest.

The next day Robert circled the camp like a starving shark, he searched the perimeter of the camp several times just looking for a weakening in the village forces, he searched gate after gate until he found something, a small hole, most likely made by past intruders. In a blink of an eye he wriggled himself through the tiny hole, like a worm attempting to get to the surface. But he made a lot of noise! The guards were alerted!

Frantically, he got his trembling hands on the nearest weapon, it was a wooden plank with rusty nails imbedded within, making it a lethal weapon. Roberto stood there as waves of men with intimidating muscles ran at him, he looked like he could take on the world, he kept fighting group after group, conceding various painful injuries, but his adrenalin kicked in, disabling him from feeling anything, brutally killing anyone in the range of his weapon. After slaughtering the majority of the village army they surrendered and Roberto heard that familiar voice once again, it was the village leader!

With a smile on his face Roberto and the village leader travelled the land slowly making their way back to the village (home). After a seemingly long two days the village was in sight, it was a glorious sight for the both of them.

They strutted down the path leading into the village like soldiers coming home from war, everyone rushed to greet them they were back and now Roberto was   truly   a   hero.

Tornalis' Adventure

by Zach Johnson

Over the moon with what they discovered on the Isle of Man, Tornalis hastily leapt off the longboat – which was carrying tons of gold and silver – he was delighted to be back home. Exhausted, he laid on the soft blanket sand. An unpleasant scent of manure wafted in the air. There was a smell of charred wood in the warmth of the campfires, as plumes of smoke could be seen in the sky. Digging up the sand, there was something very solid; a hammer.

"Whoa! Dad, look what I found!" called Tornalis.

"Keep it safe," dad whispered to him.

Tornalis picked it up and a bolt of lightning shot up into the air.

Moments later, Tornalis noticed a Saxon boat coming; it was a raid…

Lost for words, Tornalis froze in horror to the sight of an enemy army coming to shore. Running now, Tornalis didn't dare look back, screaming for attention. The Saxons had arrived. A brigade of pig-faced men hoarded the island. Tornalis ran home but the door was locked. Left to die, Tornalis curled up in a ball, commotion tugging on his ear drums. One Saxon came to Tornalis and flung him across the path.

"OW!" Tornalis wailed in pain.

The villainous warrior took the hammer.

"Got it! HAHA!" the corrupt pig shouted, laughing in Tornalis' face. He ran off as the cruel Anglo-Saxons sailed away.

"Oh no! The hammer!" Tornalis cried.

He had to get it back. Feeling ashamed, he told everyone to get on the longboat. Away from shore, a Briton boat was in vision. Everyone froze. What were they doing coming to their island? With little hope after the last battle they steered away but the Britons followed. They had no choice, time to fight.

"Give us our hammer back!" they demanded.

'It was their hammer?!' Tornalis thought to himself. Suddenly, BOOM!! Their first cannon fired. Wood scattered into the water; they'd been hit! Slowly, the boat felt off balance; they were sinking!

"Dad! Dad! Dad! DAD!" Tornalis yelled, tears streaming down his cheeks.

"We're sinking!".

Another cannon fired. CRASH!! The Britons finally rushed in, chuckling to themselves. But then they quickly realized they didn't have the hammer.

"RUN TORNALIS!" Dad screamed.

"RUN!".

Tornalis stayed put.

"No Dad. If I want to be a successful Viking Leader, I must help," Tornalis explained.

A few seconds later, they were met by water.

"Fine, I'll go," Tornalis exclaimed, crying.

With that, he jumped into the sea as his dad was being fought to the death.

"GOOOO…" Dad's screams were cut as he was hit in the chest.

Now the boat was fully emerged in the water. Tornalis must avenge him; but how? After a while of swimming, there was a shadowy figure... a shark?!

With his heart pounding out of his chest and his mind racing, Tornalis thought of his end.

"Please don't see me," he murmured.

Suddenly, the silhouette flashed and teleported. What's happening? It was getting close now. Soon, it could be seen in detail. Blood painted its jagged teeth red. Part of its top fin was ripped off and it had a jaw larger than a deer. Tornalis backed away, still coming. The creature opened its mouth revealing a Saxon warrior; dead. With quick thinking, Tornalis jumped up and ripped its top jaw open.

"Got to get the meat," Tornalis mumbled.

After a while, a dolphin showed up holding a map. Tornalis realized it was the Anglo-Saxon base.

"Take me there!" Tornalis demanded.

"I need my hammer."

Resting on the dolphin's back, he stared at the map.

"Thank you," Tornalis pleaded.

"I'm going to keep you as a pet; I'll name you Wayne, okay?"

Wayne leapt into the air in happiness.

"Cool, oh! That's the island!" Tornalis announced.

"No one here!" he noticed.

"They must be on a raid."

Tornalis swiftly sprinted through the village to the monastery which was storing the hammer.

"Gotcha!"

As he turned around, he saw that the Saxons had come back.

"Hey fellas!" Tornalis greeted them.

"Looking a bit weaker!"

"Well, well, well if it isn't the wannabe Viking," called the Saxon Leader.

"Ha, very funny," Tornalis shot back sarcastically.

"You ready?"

"Ready for what?" they replied.

"You'll see," Tornalis answered with a smirk. BANG!!

"ARGH!" they screamed as a bolt of lightning hit their boat.

Tornalis smiled.

"Who's weak now?" Tornalis shouted.

"We're sorry!" the Saxons apologized.

"Too late now cowards!" Tornalis told them.

The enemies charged. BOOM!! More lightning. Hit after hit, Tornalis was too powerful for them. Soon enough, it was only the leader remaining. BAM!! He laid there in flames; dead. He'd done it. Tornalis had reclaimed the hammer in victory. Suddenly, his fellow Vikings came to celebrate with him, including his parents.

"Dad! I thought you'd died!" Tornalis spoke.

"No, I killed them," Dad announced.

"Mum?" Tornalis was confused.

"I was taken away by Loki but I made it out," Mum explained.

A roar of cheers went up. Tornalis ran to Wayne and hugged him. "Thank you so much!" Tornalis acknowledged him.

"He brought me a map which guided me here; He's a legend," Tornalis stated. "Odin bless you."

Printed in Great Britain
by Amazon